Tuesdays at Charlie's

Fermanagh Creative Writing Group

Fermanagh Creative Writing Group wish to thank:

Fermanagh District Council for their financial help in producing this anthology

and – of course – the Burns family and the staff of Charlie's Bar.

Published 2012

by

Fermanagh Creative Writing Group

ISBN 878-1-907530-26-5

Editing: Gordon Williams
Proof-reading: Tony Brady, Dianne Trimble, Anthony Viney

Cover design: Ken Ramsey and Sarah Wieghell

Foreword

What happens on Tuesdays at Charlie's? It's a bar, so there are people meeting, talking, drinking. And at half past seven, Fermanagh time, people gather in the quiet back room – meeting, talking, drinking.

And reading what they've written: stories, memoirs, commentaries, articles. Whatever takes them. They even allow some poetry. Things that are important enough to write about: humour, tragedy, romance. Fact, fiction and pieces that blur those boundaries. Stories of growing up and growing old. Pieces of life, death and the bits in between.

Some weeks there are visiting writers giving tutorials; every week there is advice and support: discussing what has been written and how to improve it. Some members are starting to write; others have been writing for years. This anthology is a selection of what we've read in Charlie's back room.

New members are always welcome. We'll see you on Tuesdays at Charlie's.

Contents

2

3

My First Performance

PETER BYRNE

Sunday afternoon came; I'd been practicing all week and I thought I had a good chance. Me and my best pal Joey arrived at the Picture House. It was only one o'clock but already the queue was a mile long. We walked past all the other boys and girls; most of them I didn't recognize, they must have been from other housing estates. I overheard one boy say to his friend, "Would you look who's coming - it's Laurel and Hardy in person."

They both started laughing. Lucky that Joey didn't hear them, or there would have been a scrap. Here and there between ones laughing, fighting and messing, there were others getting their last practice in before the competition. Me and Joey went to the back of the queue. I took my yoyo out of my pocket and started practicing, too.

"D'you think you have a good chance, Peewee?"

"Don't know, Joey. Some of them are good, aren't they?"

"Yeah - did you see the fella in the blue jumper, walking the dog?"

"I did."

"He was good, wasn't he?"

"Yeah, he was."

While I was busy practicing, Joey had to make himself busy, too. There was a bunch of girls in front of us, and he kept tugging at the ponytail of one of them. Every time she turned round, she'd give him a dirty look, but Joey had his hands in his pockets whistling up at the sky.

"What will you do with the money if you win, Peewee?"

"I'll give you £1 and me ma £2 and keep two for myself."

"I hope you win, Peewee," Joey said.

People said that me and Joey were like brothers, because we went everywhere together. Some said, behind our backs, that we were like Laurel and Hardy, because Joey was pudgy and I was skinny and we were always fooling around, but today we were trying to be serious, or at least I was.

A man in a wine-coloured jacket and jet black hair shining with Brylcreem walked up and down the queue. He was telling everyone to get

5

in line. Every now and then he'd stop at some girls, stick his face in theirs, put his torch to his mouth and sing Elvis songs. Some off the girls blushed, but most just laughed at him.

At last the queue started to move, but after a few steps it stopped. Then it moved again and stopped again, and moved and stopped. Eventually I could see the woman in the ticket box. She had a moustache and jam jar glasses and her eyes were massive. I was glad Joey hadn't noticed her. Elvis was stabbing the queue with his torch, letting a bunch in at a time, to pay for their tickets and disappear into the picture house. Me and Joey were in the top bunch now, and Elvis was shouting over our heads.

"Have your money ready, boys and girls."

I felt in my pocket with one hand for the two thruppenny bits my ma give me, still practicing on my yoyo with my other. There wasn't much room, because we were all tightly bunched up, and when my yoyo was spinning up the cord, it got caught under the dress of the girl with the ponytail, pulling her dress up so we could see her knickers. She turned around and gave me a box in the ear and called me a little shit.

"Hey, you," Elvis roared, pointing his torch at me. "Stop your messing."

"It was an accident," I shouted, rubbing my ear.

The girl squealed. "Hey, mister, he put his hand up my dress."

"Who did?"

"Him," she said, pointing her finger in my face.

"I did not, it was me yoyo."

Joey had his hand pressed to his mouth, but it didn't stop him laughing.

"You and you, get to the back of the queue."

"Ah Jasus, mister, it was an accident," I shouted.

"Don't you curse at me, you little shite. Get to the back of the queue."

Me and Joey were last in line again but when no one was looking, we skipped up the queue. When we got to the top again, Elvis stabbed the air in front of us. "Have your money ready, boys and girls," he shouted.

Me and Joey were looking up at the woman with the jam jar glasses now; she was chewing on a sweet and it must have been a toffee, because her false teeth were locked together and moving in the opposite direction to her jaws. I was trying to stop from laughing, but then Joey stuck his face in mine with his eyes crossways in his head. I done the same back at him, and we both broke into fits. Then we heard a voice behind us.

"Hey mister, them two skipped the queue."

Elvis pointed his torch at us. "Who - these two?"

"Yeah, mister."

"We didn't mister, honest," we blurted together at his torch with our innocent altar boy look.

"Get to the back."

"But mister....."

"Get to the back of the queue, you little shites."

It was half two when me and Joey were in our seats at the back of the picture house. It was packed, and noisier than the zoo at feeding time. Everyone was sucking on ice-pops and drinking minerals and throwing popcorn and shouting and roaring and jumping up and down in their seats. Then suddenly everything went dark and everyone went quiet, except for a squeal from a girl, who must have had her bum pinched. Then a searchlight made a round bright spot on the stage, and a little man appeared in the middle of it. He looked like Charlie Chaplin, except he didn't have a cane and he could talk.

"Boys and girls, before the matinee today we have the little matter of the yoyo competition. The prize is £5 for the winner, so anyone who wants to take part will they come up to the stage now?"

The moment I'd been waiting on had arrived. I jumped out of my seat and fought my way through a row of knees and feet, getting pushed and shoved and cursed at as I went. Free now, I ran down the side isle and climbed the high steps onto the stage, passing under the eyes of Elvis and the beam off his torch. There were twenty five boys and girls lined up across the stage. Charlie Chaplin stood in front of us, with his back to the audience: he was giving us instructions as we were showing off our skills. The first tricks were easy, then they got harder and harder. Anytime someone made a mistake, they were disqualified and sent back to their seats to a huge cheer.

It wasn't long till there was only five left, and I hadn't made a mistake. Then Charlie Chaplin shouted, "Walk the dog."

7

For this trick, you had to hold your yoyo tight in your fist, and bending your arm so your fist was touching your shoulder, throw down your arm and opening your hand, flick the yoyo over your fingers, making it unwind down the cord and spin along the floor while you walked beside it.

After walking the dog, two of us were told to sit down. That only left me and a girl, and the boy in the blue jumper. Then Charlie Chaplin looked at his watch and announced that the next trick was to be the last, and whoever won would get the £5 prize money. Then he shouted, "Criss cross."

Great, I thought, this was my favourite. To do this trick, you had to flick your yoyo out at chest level and let it unravel to the end of the cord, then jerk it back up the cord towards your left shoulder, then out again and back again towards your right shoulder, making an "X" in the air. Whoever made the most Xs would be the winner. I'd learned the secret of this trick - the harder I flung my yoyo out at the beginning, the more Xs it made. Once, I'd done eight, but that was in practice.

The girl went first, but she only managed four. Then it was the turn of the boy in the blue jumper, and he only managed five. Now it was my turn. I could already feel the crispy £5 in my back pocket, so I took my time to enjoy the moment I'd been waiting on. I could see my best pal Joey at the back; he had his fingers in his mouth, whistling louder than anyone else. Then I heard booing coming from the front row: it was the girl with the ponytail who boxed me in the ear earlier, but I hadn't come this far to be put off by a whinger like her. So I closed my eyes for a second to concentrate......Now I was ready. As hard as I could, I let fly. My red and yellow yoyo left my hand at the speed of light - this was the start I needed. Then I felt a snap and the string flew back and landed on my nose, but my yoyo was still travelling through the air. Then I heard a scream - someone in the front row was holding their head. It was the girl with the ponytail. Charlie Chaplin jumped off the stage, nearly breaking his leg, and limped over to see if the girl was okay.

I was going to do a runner, but it was too late. I got the smell of Brylcreem from behind me and I felt me jumper tighten around me neck. Raised off the stage, I was dangling in mid air.

"It was an accident," I gaggled.

"You're an accident," Elvis roared.

Carrying me up the aisle, he didn't drop me down till we were outside on the pavement. Sitting on the kerb on my own, without even a stray dog for company, I was feeling sorry for myself. A cheer went up from inside the picture house: it must have been for the boy in the blue jumper. It should have been for me. Then I heard a door opening behind me; when I looked around, I could see my best pal Joey travelling by air, too.

"You two are barred," Elvis shouted, landing Joey on his arse on the ground beside me.

"What did I do?" Joey grumbled

"You're guilty by association," Elvis said, before he disappeared back into the picture house.

I didn't know what association meant, but at least I wasn't alone now.

Sitting with our heads in our knees, listening to the roars of laughter coming from the picture house, where Laurel and Hardy were performing now, I felt a tap on my shoulder. When I turned my head, Joey was doing his Oliver Hardy impersonation. Twiddling his invisible tie, he said, "That's another fine mess you got me into."

Holding back my tears, I dangled the limp cord on my finger, while I fumbled my hair with my other hand, and did the best Stan Laurel impression ever.

With that me and Joey broke into fits of laughing, louder than all the laughter behind us.

Entertainment

KEN RAMSEY

Early on a hot late 1950's summer evening the Mill Street Gang were lazing in the gang H.Q., a commandeered sandbag guard hut behind the power transformers. We had nothing to do. We were bored and needed entertainment. No one had any ideas, leastways ideas that we had not done before and now we were too bored to do any of them again.

"There's a film called *Horror of Dracula* in the Ritz Cinema," said Tony. "It's about a vampire who attacks people and sucks out all their blood." Now everyone was paying attention. Tony's big brother worked in the Ritz and knew all about films, especially the scary horror films. He took great delight in describing them in all their gory detail to Tony, who always relayed the stories to the gang.

We were not allowed into the cinema to watch horror films because none of us was sixteen: if you were under sixteen it was against the law to watch horror films. There was the challenge, all in the words 'against the law', 'horror', 'vampires', 'blood'.

None of us in the Mill Street gang had ever seen a horror film. We knew about them; knew how frightening they were. We had heard about audiences cringing and screaming with fear. Victor's mother had sat through the *Curse of Frankenstein* with her eyes closed tight all the time. His father had to hold on to her to stop her fleeing out of the cinema. Even the words *Frankenstein* and *Dracula* were frightening. We were so excited that the latest one - *The Horror of Dracula* - was in our cinema in Technicolor and Sensurround sound. We were all abuzz and making plans. The Ritz cinema was in our gang territory and we would have no difficulty getting even fourteen of us inside – without paying of course.

"Right," said Leo, our gang leader. "Here's the plan: Tony, you'll climb up and get in through the toilet window and we'll all wait outside at the front emergency exit door until you sneak down and open it". Timing was crucial; the films started at seven o'clock with advertisements followed by the Pathe News reel, then the trailers for the next films, more advertisements then a break before the main film. We spent a few minutes perfecting our entry plan even though we had used it many times before to sneak into the cinema. Leo strutted in front of us like a General in a war movie as he detailed everyone's role in our plan to invade the cinema to watch the forbidden *Horror of Dracula* for free.

At the agreed time we all set off from the gang hut; we ran across the Convent field up into the Forthill Gardens and down to the back of the cinema. Leo and Victor kept watch for anyone looking out of the cinema owner's house. On Leo's signal five of us ran forward, three of us hurried up to the wall below the toilet window and braced ourselves with arms out against the wall. Two more followed, climbed up on our shoulders and leaned against the wall. Tony clambered over all of us to reach the open window and squirmed through into the cinema. The rest of us melted back into the Forthill Gardens. We ran down onto the main street round to the front emergency door of the cinema and waited, all trying to look as innocent as the Pope.

Meanwhile, Tony sneaked out of the toilet and into the cinema. Under the cover of the dark and the flickering lights he ran, ducked down, to the front seats and settled unseen in one of them. At the end of the trailers and before the start of the big picture there were more adverts, cinemagoers shuffled about buying drinks and ice cream and going to the toilet. This was Tony's moment: he scrambled down along the floor hidden by the front seats, crawled under the very heavy blackout curtain in front of the emergency exit and down the short corridor and pushed the emergency exit door open. We all crowded in, temporarily filling the corridor with bright sunlight, but the heavy curtain did its job and not a chink of light showed in the cinema. Leo closed the door tight. From the dim corridor we began one after the other to sneak under the curtain and fill all the seats of the front row just eight or ten feet from the enormous screen above us. We were all in and seated, keeping down low so as not to be noticed by the cinema staff in the flickering gloom. There was no one behind us for ten rows so they didn't need to go down to the front row.

The film started - *The Horror of Dracula* began to unfold directly above us. We watched wide-eyed as, in the film, darkness fell into a black night and a young man arrived outside the grim foreboding Dracula Castle towering chillingly above us. Our eyes opened wide with fear. After banging the front door he was led into the candlelit library room. Christopher Lee acting as Count Dracula entered. We became even more fearful when Count Dracula took the young man to a bedroom and locked him in there. A beautiful young girl tried to help him escape by unlocking the door, then kissed him and sank long fangs into his neck. We knew he was doomed to be a vampire. Before he could escape Count Dracula appeared as if by magic - his teeth and long white fangs were dripping blood. He killed the young man and, scooping up the girl, he flew out of the window into the night, his long cloak becoming vampire's wings.

The Mill Street Gang in the front row cowered underneath Dracula on the huge screen. We were unable to move, all paralysed with fear. No one dared breathe or blink as Dracula towered right above and around us. Blood dripped down on top of us as he bit the men's necks and did terrible things to all the women, before biting their necks until everyone was a vampire. By now we were shaking with terror, speechless with horror and hanging on to each other for dear life.

Then the good guy appeared, Doctor Van Helsing played by Peter Cushing. He hunted down and killed vampires, but he didn't ease our fear, he made it worse - much worse. He took out crucifixes and began burning vampires. When he caught Dracula sleeping in a coffin he got a wooden pointed stake from his leather bag and set it over Dracula's chest. Then over his head he raised a huge mallet to drive down the stake into Dracula's heart.

I don't know who bolted first, but before the doctor could strike the blow to kill Dracula, the petrified Mill Street Gang were in full flight fighting like a pack of rats to get out through the heavy dark curtain and down the corridor and out of the cinema. The entire gang charged into the emergency doors just as Dracula screamed. The doors crashed open and we all tumbled out convinced Dracula was behind us. The sudden white glare of the evening sunlight blinded us. The terror was total - we were in a pitched battle with Dracula and we were losing. Tears, snot and slobber were choking us as we squabbled like a ball of cats - biting, punching and kicking anything near us. It took a long time for us to calm down and flee back to the gang headquarters. We cowered in the hut, eventually someone said, "Jasus," and every one of us burst into a gaggle of every curse word we knew - all except Benny, his uncle was a priest. It was a good hour later, but before it got dark, when we were ready to go home.

This had been the greatest adventure and the best entertainment the gang had ever had, but none of us slept in the dark for many weeks after *The Horror of Dracula*.

Two Gentlemen of Stepney

TONY BRADY

I have met some famous people but the most infamous people I ever met were the Krays.

I helped out at London's Repton club – a boys' youth club that specialised in boxing – in the 1960s. The club staged an annual Gala Boxing Night to raise funds and showcase its boxing talent and much of the East End society attended.

I wasn't keen on boxing but I went along because I'd been invited. Inside the club I was spotted by the warden, George Layton, who introduced me to the Committee, seated at a corner table. I could barely see the other guests through the cigar and cigarette smoke: the cup and purse sponsors seated at the other raised corner tables. During the interval the standing room only crowd were watching the youngest club members, in white vests and baggy shorts, who entertained them with sparring feints and punching the padded fists of their trainers.

George summoned a squat, heavily built man nearby and said I should meet two ex-members who were there. He spoke to the man whose face showed the evidence of much boxing experience: he reminded me of Odd-Job in the James Bond film *Goldfinger*. He wore a bow tie and looked oriental because of the punches his face had taken when boxing at the highest level. Odd-Job silently beckoned me to follow him through the crowd which parted before him as he led me to another corner table where six men sat. The nearest was watching the young boys in the ring, moving his body in unison with theirs, not allowing us to distract him. Then Odd-Job leaned over and said, "Ronnie, Reggie – this is Tony. Ee's awright. A genelman."

I shook hands with Ronnie who stared past me at the ring. Then I shook Reggie's outstretched hand. "George," he said, indicating a man wearing a fedora hat, and I shook his hand, too. Then a voice boomed, "Boothby," as a greeting and its owner shook my hand. A bell sounded and a fanfare announced the next bout on the bill. As there was no available space at that table Odd-Job led me back to my original place.

Throughout the evening the people at my table told me who I had been introduced to: Odd-Job had been a professional boxer who had started at the Repton club. Ronnie and Reggie Kray were also Repton old boys, having learned to box there in their teens. They later became infamous for their violent criminal activities. The Kray Twins were also great fans of gangster movies and their guest "George" was George Raft – the Hollywood actor who specialised in gangster roles, often as a gentleman killer. And "Boothby" was Lord Boothby, old Etonian and bisexual Conservative peer, whose association with the Krays may have protected their criminal activities from being publicised in the media and being investigated by the police.

All at the Kray's table got up to present prizes to the winners of the evening's contests – money contributed by the paying public and distinguished guests.

The club had been set up in the nineteenth century and promoted by Repton public school in Northamptonshire. Then, boys and masters had spent their long summer holidays living in the impoverished East End, working as social missionaries to foster "muscular Christianity" through clean living, godliness and the noble art of boxing.

The Kray Twins became part of East End criminal folklore and were sometimes favourably cast: it's said that they loved their mother and were kind to old ladies. Having met them I was intrigued by the observation: "The Krays were real gentlemen; they never killed anyone without being introduced to them first!"

Going Home

DIANNE TRIMBLE

Karen put her slippers into the suitcase. They were always one of the last items she packed. She checked her purse again to be sure her ticket and passport were there. It didn't hurt to double check. The clock on the dresser said two o'clock. Still three hours until she had to leave.

Karen always hated the last day of her visit home. Every year she spent the day dreading the parting to come. She would wander back and forth between her old bedroom, still painted her favourite delicate shade of yellow, and the living room, making sure she had packed everything. The hours dragged until she headed off to the airport for her flight to Belfast. The last day always passed slower than any other day of her holiday.

She made an annual trip to Toronto and there was never enough time to see everyone she wanted to, visit all the familiar places she loved and spend enough time with her family. As each day of her holiday passed she marked it off in her mind. One day closer to leaving. It hung over her for her entire stay. Now that the day was here she wished all the goodbyes were over.

"I'm making tea. Would you like a cup?" her mother called from the kitchen.

"Thanks. I'll be there in a minute," Karen replied.

She closed the lid of the suitcase and wandered down the hall, her sandals slapping the cream tiles as she walked. She stopped at the living room doorway, studying the familiar room and its furnishings, cluttered and comfortable. Her mother's glass animal figurines perched on handmade pine tables either end of the worn, saggy sofa. As a child, standing eye level to the tables, she had played with the miniature figures, moving them across the shiny wood surfaces, careful not to let them slip off and break.

She flopped into an armchair, leaned her head back against its frayed corduroy fabric and studied the painting opposite that had always fascinated her. The scene was a nineteenth century English library or drawing room, filled with mahogany bookshelves and highly polished tables. The room's huge French window was wide open, its panels flung outwards to reveal a calm harbour dotted with sailing boats beyond.

She had always imagined herself curled up in the deep-buttoned, brown leather armchair in that drawing room, gazing out at the harbour. Her mind would race, imagining all the places those boats might be destined for: across the Atlantic to a scorching Caribbean island or in the opposite direction to the Old World - maybe France or Spain.

"This time tomorrow you'll be home again," her mother said, setting down the cup of tea beside her. Karen's eyes jerked away from the painting to her mother. She tried to compose her face and hide her shock. This cramped, red brick bungalow was her home. When she wandered from room to room all her childhood memories flooded back. She had never lived anywhere except Toronto before she moved to Ireland. How could her mother talk about going home?

For months before she arrived in Toronto each year she imagined tasting pancakes smothered in maple syrup at the Farmer's Market on Saturday mornings, feeling the breeze hitting her face as she stood on the open deck of the ferry crossing to Centre Island and seeing the wonderful displays that vied for attention in the downtown shop windows. Memories of her hometown filled her head all year and her excitement grew as winter's hold receded and the date of her next visit home came closer.

At the end of her first trip downtown each year, when she finally trooped out of the glass domed Eaton Centre laden with bags and collapsed onto a seat on the streetcar, she felt like she had never been away. How could her own mother suggest anywhere else was her home?

Before she had booked this trip John suggested that they might have an extended vacation this year, maybe to New Zealand or Africa. But she didn't have enough leave from work to do both and she wouldn't miss coming home. So she had told him to put the idea on hold. Maybe they could do it in a year or two.

"John'll have missed you. He'll be glad to have you home," her mother continued. Karen winced at the mention of Ireland as home again. She thought of John on his own in their end terrace Belfast house. The slightly dilapidated brick house looked much like every other house in the row but their front window was framed by the deep burgundy curtains that she had made a couple years ago and she thought they made it stand out from the others. Many houses on the street were being renovated and the neighbourhood looked much tidier than when they'd first moved in.

Before she had left, spring had come in bright and mild. She was a bit surprised to feel the nip in the breeze when she arrived in Toronto; she'd forgotten that spring arrived several weeks later here than in Belfast.

Karen thought of John: he would be busy cutting the grass, weeding and planting new shrubs in the border of the tiny, square plot of ground that was their front garden.

Their grey tabby cat would be lying in the sun near him as he worked, sometimes standing up and stretching. She wasn't nearly as active as she had been as a kitten. She would move just enough to loosen up, then flop onto her side on the footpath's warm pavement again. Maybe, while Karen had been away, John might have made the flower boxes that he had been talking about for the past seven or eight years, the ones that always deferred to some more urgent project.

Is it really seven or eight years since we decided that flower boxes would be the perfect touch for our front windows? It can't be that long, Karen thought, surprised. But they had decided to make them before any of their neighbours had begun renovations. Now that she thought about it, they'd bought the house ten years ago, soon after John had asked her to move to Ireland and marry him.

"What's your book club reading?" her mother asked.

"*Number 5* by Glenn Patterson. It's about the lives of successive owners of a house in Belfast." Karen had the book packed in her hand luggage to read on the flight.

"Sounds interesting. I'm sure you'll enjoy reading a book that's set where you live. How's everyone at the club?" her mother asked.

"The same as ever," Karen replied, rolling her eyes with a mock sigh. Her friends in the book club were all outspoken and opinionated. Amicable disagreements were often part of their discussions. She always left meetings in good spirits.

18

Anne'll likely drop by before the next meeting. We'll have a chance to chat and catch up. Karen smiled at the thought. She had lots to tell Anne after two weeks away.

"Don't forget to give Iris the peanut butter cookies. She really liked the ones I brought over last year." Her mother's voice interrupted Karen's thoughts.

"I have them in my hand luggage so they won't get crushed," Karen replied. "I'll probably see her at the weekend. We often go round for Sunday lunch."

Karen thought of her calm, soft spoken mother-in-law. She had felt welcome at her mother-in-law's white-washed, two-storey farmhouse from the early days, soon after she had moved to Ireland, when she was still treated as a guest and not allowed to help with anything. Whenever she visited back then she would be given a seat beside the imposing oak mantelpiece where the heat from the open peat fire stung her knees and forced her to inch away from it. She would stare at her reflection in the floral patterned tiles set in the surround as John's sisters bustled from the Aga cooker to the sink, draining large pots and dishing their contents onto plates. Now she joined in the chaos of preparing the meal and pitched in with the washing up afterwards like everyone else in the family.

Karen looked at the painting opposite her again. She had always loved the feeling she got when she imagined herself in the scene. The armchair in the painting seemed a safe vantage point from which to view the world. In its shelter she would be cradled safely, with a world of possibilities before her. Her mother followed her gaze.

"You used to stare at that painting for ages when you were a child. I see you still like it. Why don't you take it for your living room?"

"You've had it for so long. I couldn't," Karen protested.

"Nonsense. I've been thinking of re-decorating and a couple new paintings would freshen the place up a bit. It would really suit your home."

Her mother had said it again. Your home. Karen thought about it. Belfast and that end terrace house really were her home now.

Her husband and her friends were there. Her life was there. She would love to have her favourite painting in her living room – in her home. It would hang above her pine mantelpiece where she could flop onto their

19

burgundy leather sofa and gaze at it. Leaving didn't seem as hard when she knew she really was going home.

Karen set down her tea cup. "Do you have some cardboard and string I could use to wrap it, Mom? I want to get it home safe."

From a Distance

DERMOT MAGUIRE

My father keeps his old shotgun behind the bathroom door, leaning against the wall beside mother's ironing board. It is hard to the touch and its barrels are cold and dark. When I dare to lift it up its weight intimidates me. The stock is a chestnut brown and the metal around it has swirly carvings on both sides - an old style Spanish shotgun, my father said. The two hammers stick up like the ears of a big hippo I have seen in a picture book. In the kitchen there is an old framed sepia photo of my granda with a dog, and this gun under his arm. My father keeps his cartridges in the old black swan on the high shelf in the scullery. He shoots the crows that come to eat the apples in the orchard and, in the winter time, he comes home with mallard ducks and magnificent cock pheasants.

As I get older the shotgun seems to get lighter and I can even lift it up to my shoulder. Then I pull the hammer back, line up the barrels in the mirror, pull the trigger and, click, shoot myself right between the eyes. Sometimes I imagine I am shooting grumpy old Smokey, our maths teacher, or sarcastic Specs, our Irish teacher. I begin to wonder what it must be like to pull the trigger and fire a cartridge. It becomes a secret obsession.

So, one Saturday in September 1964, when I'm fourteen and the rest of the family have gone into town, I stand on a chair to get a cartridge out of the black swan, take the shotgun, break it down, put the cartridge in the right barrel and go stealthily around the gable of the house into the orchard. The crows are up in the apple trees. I ease my way over to the shelter of the old spreading yew and wait for a crow to come within range.

I wait and watch. My father has said that anything more than forty yards is too far. The palms of my hands become sticky. I think of the kick back that he has talked about. Would it break my shoulder? I rehearse it all in my mind: I must take a firm grip of the barrels, hold the stock tight against my shoulder, get my jaw right down against the butt and get my eye lined up with the little sight between the far ends of the barrels. Suddenly three or four crows land high up in an apple tree. Smokey's

21

geometry flits across my excited brain – angles, distances, my father's forty yards - no more. It looks about right. Just one of the crows is visible – swaying gently, out on a thin branch near the top. As I put the gun to my shoulder and line up the barrels on the crow my arms feel weak and my heart is pounding. The crow is in my sights now - a black, bobbing blob in the distance. I pull the trigger. The bang is like an explosion in my ears. The kickback throws me against the yew and a twinge goes through my shoulder. The frantic flapping of dozens of frightened crows taking off out through the branches adds to the sense of tumult and in the middle of it all I follow the crow falling and falling, down through the branches. Down and down to the ground. Dead! I haven't missed after all - I have shot my first bird. Then the eerie calm as the cawing of the scarpering crows fades away into the fields. I can feel the pain in my shoulder but I'm not bothered: I have fired my first shot and I've hit the target. I've done something grown-up.

Recovering myself, and tingling with satisfaction, I race over to claim my trophy. But the crow isn't dead: he's lying sideways with the upper wing outstretched and one of his legs broken. I know I have to finish him off. He has his thick beak open and his dark shiny eye blinks. I lift him in both hands and feel the warmth of his body and his heartbeat racing; his feathers are so smooth. His eye is dark and deep and so alive. Suddenly, I have no desire to kill him. As I'm looking in his eye and feeling the warmth of his sleek feathers I know that I couldn't kill him. But I know I should, even if it's only to put him out of his pain. Could he survive? His limp wing still has some traction in it. The leg is cleanly broken – it would need a splint put on it. But could he survive? Instinctively, I head towards the henhouse and place him in a laying box. The gun has to go back in the bathroom. Then I set about making the splints for the broken leg as fast as I can before the others came back from town. I find it very difficult but there is no other way. I get the job done as best I can and leave a bowl of water beside the poor thing. Throughout the evening I look in on him, bringing him bread but he doesn't move and he doesn't eat any of it. Then I try him with a worm, but still he doesn't move or eat. I know he won't survive without water.

The first thing I do the next morning when I get up is to sneak out and have a look at my bird. He is dead – cold and stiff in the box. My brothers find me out and laugh at me, and at the pathetic bandage, and call me a sissy for trying to save a stupid, vermin crow.

Danny O'Neill

MARIETTE CONNOR

Danny O'Neill was looking for a wife. Just a plain, simple, straightforward wife. There was just one proviso - she had to be rich. He sat behind the driver of the Shamrock Coach Tour as it trundled its way around Ballsbridge hotels picking up the tourists who were due to spend the day visiting the beauties of Wicklow. A brief stop at the various hotels soon had the bus full. Men in chequered pants and soft cotton hats, their partners in floral dresses and white Cuban heeled shoes, all of them carrying cameras and video recorders, the American accents far outweighing any others. The ones who interested Danny, though, were the unattached ladies....and there were quite a few of them. One in particular had caught his eye and he was aware that she wasn't averse to sharing a seat and coffee with him on the previous tours last week. He was looking forward to meeting Connie Dysart again and had been planning the evening he hoped they would spend together when the bus deposited them back at Ballsbridge.

Sure enough, he got a cheery wave and, with a, "Hi there, Danny," Connie collapsed into the seat beside him. A heavy smell of Diorissimo fought a losing battle with Danny's Calvin Klein and soon they were chattering away as the bus left Dublin and headed out on the road towards Bray. Danny thought that all his birthdays and Christmases had come together. Here he was sitting beside a fairly attractive widow from Boston. What if her eyes bulged a bit and her blonde hair was a little on the thin side. Her figure might be a wee bit more than ample but he could put up with all that when he looked at the perfectly matched pearls at her throat and the sparkling diamonds on her pudgy fingers.

Connie was taking stock, too. She saw an average sized, rather plump man with a red complexion crowned by a head of luxurious white wavy hair. He sported a moustache above a set of good, strong even teeth. "His own?" she wondered briefly. Danny's Louis Copeland sports jacket and Kingston shirt with regimental tie were most impressive. Though Connie had never heard of the Royal Irish Hussars, she never for a moment thought they didn't exist.

Danny knew he looked good. "God's gift to blondes and bookies," his late wife, Minnie, used to say as he set off each day on his insurance round in the northern suburbs of Dublin. He had been delighted with the jacket he'd found in the charity shop. As for the hair - well, women wore wigs: why should they have all the advantages? He patted his hair down carefully and proceeded to charm his companion with tales of leprechauns and Irish patriots.

"You know so much," Connie gushed, "about history and legends and Ireland." Danny smiled modestly and silently thanked Brother Joseph in the Christian Brothers for the history and his own fertile imagination for the legends.

They had met for the first time a week ago when Connie had dropped her passport as she boarded the bus and Danny had ruined his second best pair of trousers and banged his knee badly while retrieving it. The resultant limp had stayed with him since and gave credence to the background of a mysterious hush-hush job with government. "It's more of a desk job now," he lied to Connie, "And I don't quite know how I'll pass the time when I retire next month."

Connie and Danny spent the next two hours as a couple. They shared their memories of their partners, Connie telling her new friend about her Casper who had made a 'killing' by selling properties in Boston; and Danny, not to be outdone, had casually mentioned his army days. "Family tradition, you know," and the natural move into "something secret" in the government.

An invitation to spend some time in Boston soon followed and Danny thought that now was the time to splurge a little bit when the bus stopped at Greystones. After a stroll around the small town and a coffee, Connie spotted a tiny green ceramic frog in the window of an antique and souvenir shop. "I won't take *no* for an answer. You shall have it," was his reply to Connie's, "How sweet, but maybe too expensive."

While she repaired to the ladies' powder room in the coffee shop, Danny slipped next door and, after buying a few cards of Wicklow, left some minutes later, the cards in a paper bag and the green frog in his pocket. The shopkeeper would hardly miss it, he thought, as he clambered onto the bus and into his seat beside Connie.

Working to a strict budget, Danny was glad it had been so easy to 'pick up' the frog. This was the fourth tour he had taken recently and he was beginning to wonder if his investment would ever pay off. He knew Connie was going to London and then on to Boston in a few days. It was now or never, he thought, and decided to make his pitch that very evening.

All Danny's plans for a quiet dinner for two at a middle-of-the-road bistro in Drumcondra went by the wayside when Connie declared herself too tired to go out again. "Let's eat in the hotel here," she suggested, waving her arms towards the dining room. Only the thought that, somehow, the bill would go onto Connie's tab encouraged Danny to agree. Just in case though, he ate very sparingly and watched in horror as his lady scoffed four hearty courses from pâté through a huge sirloin to a meringue concoction. Her coffee had a wee dram in it and she looked flushed and happy. Danny felt that now was his chance. "Now or never," he thought as he leaned across the table and clasped Connie's pudgy hand in his.

"This trip to Boston," he began, "where will I stay?"

"Why, in my home," Connie smiled knowingly at him.

"New fangled ways are difficult for me. I would feel better if our relationship was more formal."

Seeing her questioning look he hurried on. "Would you be prepared to become engaged to me?"

Surprise showed in Connie's face but the clasped hands and earnest look from Danny did the trick and she lowered her eyes in a way she had long practised under the mistaken idea that looking this way, half smiling, made her look like the late Princess Diana.

"Why Danny, how romantic. But you must let me think about this. My Casper always told me to sleep on decisions of importance. Still, you are such great company… and the beautiful frog," she opened her eyes and again noted with pleasure the lovely head of white hair, the gleaming teeth of her companion. Her friends in Boston would be so impressed and well….life could be lonely for a fifty-nine year old widow, no matter how rich. Connie skirted quickly over the fact that she was well into the

26

heavenly side of sixty. Fluttering her eyelashes she called the waiter. "Champagne please….a special occasion!"

Danny's hand fastened convulsively around Connie's. He couldn't believe his luck - only three dates and he had clicked. He began to think feverishly of methods of getting together the fare to Boston.

The rest of the evening was exciting although expensive. Danny had to use his almost exhausted credit card to settle the bill in the hotel and although his leave taking from Connie was romantic as far as she was concerned, he was wondering if he had bitten off more than he could chew. He caught the Luas tram home and spent the journey thinking up ways and means of getting his hands on more money - and soon. Connie was due to leave for Boston in a few days and he had promised to join her as soon as he could make all the necessary arrangements. He still hadn't solved the problem when he alighted from the tram and headed down the street to his little flat.

Connie and Danny spent the following day together, wandering through Henry Street and looking at the shops. After lunch in Temple Bar, they made their way to St. Stephen's Green and sat on a seat near the pond.

"This is our last day together until I meet you in Boston." Connie tucked her arm into Danny's and gave him her *Diana* look again. "You must let me have your address and phone details, dear," she continued, "and I'll give you mine." She fished in her smart calfskin purse and produced a gilt-edged card.

"I've run out of cards….new ones at the printers," Danny mumbled, but when she insisted he scribbled his address on the back of one of hers. Danny omitted the phone number and hoped she wouldn't notice. Losing the phone because of non-payment had been a blow but surely if he got to the U.S. and married Connie all his problems would be solved and his dreams would come true? He had always been an optimist.

Only by feigning acute discomfort from the pain in his 'gammy leg' had Danny got out of paying for yet another dinner, and after a loving and tearful farewell in the foyer of the hotel, Connie went to join the rest of her tour friends and Danny made his way back home. It was nearly eleven the next morning when Danny woke to a loud knocking on his hall door.

"Who could be calling at this hour?" Then he recalled it was Sunday and immediately felt relieved. "Can't be the rent man." He got up slowly and made his way to the dingy hallway and opened the door.

"Connie!" There she was, standing on his doorstep, looking in puzzlement around the general area of St. Joseph's flats. Her eyes took in the potholes filled with the remnants of last night's rain, the empty chip wrappers flapping forlornly in the breeze and the broken Tesco trolley leaning drunkenly against the wall. She turned and saw Danny standing in the doorway. His worn T-shirt and boxer shorts covered his ample frame but her gaze lingered in amazement on his bald shining head and his sunken cheeks. He couldn't speak - shock and the fact that his teeth rested in a glass beside his bed prevented him. Connie swept past him into the flat. She flopped her shining black purse onto the table and it lay there like a dead bird.

"Dead. That's what I am now," Danny thought as he followed her into his sitting room. Still in silence, Connie looked about the room. She saw the sagging couch, the small table with the newspapers, pages turned to the racing section; the wedding photo of Danny and Minnie and overall, the layers of dust and neglect. She turned and spoke slowly. "I came to tell you that I feel all this," - she waved her hands in the air – "I mean you and me is too fast for me and we should, perhaps, give it time to develop. Get to know each other a bit more."

Danny hung his head, silent. After a long pause Connie picked up her purse from the table.

"Perhaps you'll write?" She passed him quickly as he stood in the doorway and he heard the hall door bang behind her.

In a daze, Danny put the kettle on the gas hob in the kitchen and made himself a cup of tea. He drank it slowly as the realisation of the morning's events became clear. "Well, that's that. She won't be bothering me now. Still, maybe if I go to the hotel? No, it just wouldn't work." He knew that the sight of him without his teeth and hair had been a huge shock for Connie, but maybe not as bad as seeing where and how he lived. Sipping his tea, he wandered into the sitting room. There, nestling among the racing papers and dust on the table, was the ceramic frog. He knew it was all over between Connie and him. He picked it up, turning it over speculatively in his hand. All was not lost; there was always next year; more bus tours and more eager ladies. And, in the meantime, how much he could get for the frog?

Danny O'Neill whistled as he dressed for town and headed for the pawn shop. As I said before....he was a true optimist.

Nothing Personal

ANTHONY VINEY

In Parliament today the Chancellor announced a raft of savings to the social security budget as part of the long awaited comprehensive spending review. Reductions in payments to non-working families, restrictions to housing benefit, and a rise in student tuition fees are expected to be implemented next year.

"I think you're sitting on a healthy 2.1 for this, Paul. An insightful critique on child labour in the cotton mills. Spot on.

Tracey, a brave stab at dialectical materialism, but you should try and bring yourself into the picture - as class warrior of course. Remember, Tracey, the personal is political. And Olivia - a well structured piece…but I think you're being a little too generous to Adam Smith. Read my article on Engels. You'll find it instructive."

Dr Matthew Henning, confirmed bachelor, was graced with a full head of hair that belied his years. As an early quitter from a lacklustre Campaign for Nuclear Disarmament, he had craved excitement, embracing an eclectic mix of young revolutionaries that included Che Guevara, Ulrike Meinhof and Carlos the Jackal. But for all his political acumen Dr Henning had failed to anticipate the personal body blow that arrived with the morning post.

Early retirement.

A generous pension but an unwelcome cul de sac on his path to glory. Now the 'suits' were running the show, giving *him* the heave ho and citing fiscal pressures that left them no choice. *Nothing personal.*

"Bastards."

Henning checked his notes. The last tutorial. Hard times.

At Question Time today the Shadow Chancellor condemned the increase in bankers' bonuses in the run up to Christmas. Addressing protestors outside Westminster the Head of the TUC called for further demonstrations against cuts in front line services.

Henning stretched his legs and faced the dwindling class of part-timers. Down to three and, with the exception of Paul, wholly uninspiring.

"Come on, think about it. What would dear old Karl have said about the present crisis? Paul?"

"Well, essentially it's about the ruling elite maximising profits," he replied.

Sitting opposite the young man, Henning was reminded of himself. Muscular, with close cropped hair and narrow hips, the young firebrand struck Henning as disturbingly athletic. He was bewitched.

"We only need to look at what's going on in the university," Paul continued. "Courses chopped and fees going through the roof."

"And who benefits?" asked Henning.

"The rich students. And their parents, of course," Paul answered.

"Quite," said Henning. "The university extracting maximum surplus value from the poorest students. Discarding them when they're served their purpose. The part timers now judged surplus to requirements. Redundant."

"Tracey, what's your take on this…. the cuts to welfare? Give us a Marxist perspective."

Tracey Grimshaw, evacuee from domestic violence and unwilling graduate to single parenthood, tugged at her poorly cut fringe and moved self-consciously in her chair. She struggled to relate Dr Henning's grander narrative to her own situation. On a personal level, she raged at the prospect of free classes coming to an end and little Peter losing his place in the crèche. How would she fill her time now? And how could she integrate all these individual tragedies into a broader political picture? The task seemed beyond her. For the moment she had nothing to say, but she was determined to work on it.

Henning decided against pressing the point. He could see that Tracey had difficulty with his question. Later perhaps.

"Olivia, what's the view from business class? Are you braced for a crash landing?"

Strongly perfumed and smartly trouser suited, Olivia looked up from her laptop. The newly redundant, but unrepentant, portfolio manager was

31

used to getting her own way. She disliked being quizzed by underworked academics and she had no time for hypocrites or homosexuals.

"If you really want my opinion, Dr Henning, I think you need to get real. All this claptrap about class struggle …. it's old hat. Look at China and India for God's sake. Grabbing market opportunities that you lot are happy to give away. There are no benefits for the workshy there – just hard work and solid growth. Eight percent at the last count."

"An eloquent case for fiscal responsibility," Henning replied sarcastically. "Never spending more than you earn. As every housewife knows."

Athens remains at a standstill today as workers and students engage in spontaneous street protests. The Greek Prime Minister has authorised the use of riot police to break picket lines and ensure the movement of essential supplies.

Henning drew closer to Paul as the student scanned his notes. He considered, for a moment, whether he should ask Paul to remain after class. Maybe suggest a quiet drink. He hoped that Paul would make the first move.

"So let's keep the home fires burning," he said. "Move the debate on a little. In the words of Lenin, to ask ourselves, 'What is to be done?'"

Rocking on his chair Paul spoke first. "It's like you said last week, Dr Henning. We need to focus on the new owners of the means of production. See how we can stop them moving capital to different markets and leaving working people on the scrapheap."

Henning's eyes settled again on the young man's taut figure. Paul's back was finely arched, exposing an unblemished midriff.

"So Paul, what *is* to be done?"

"It's obvious: we have to fight back. Take what's ours by any means necessary."

"By any means necessary. That's the key isn't it?" Henning said. "Now, all of you, I want you to think about this carefully. A hundred years ago our Bolshevik friends had no difficulty selecting their targets: factory owners, landlords and the Tsar, of course. But in Britain today, is it quite so

32

simple? Somebody must take responsibility. Somebody must be to blame. So, who will be the first for the firing squad?"

"Is it the bankers?" Tracey asked nervously.

"You've been doing your homework, Tracey," Henning replied approvingly. "So, how would *you* deal with the bankers, Tracey? Remember what I said earlier about the personal as political."

"I'm not sure, Dr Henning," she replied. "Should I close down my account?"

"I'm not sure that the loss of your high interest super saver will keep the City awake at night. Can you think of something more direct? More permanent?"

"Dr Henning," Olivia interrupted. "What are you suggesting? That it's OK to murder a banker?"

"Why not," said Paul. "It's those bastards that got us into this hole. I say make an example of one of them. It would beat all this hot air in Parliament."

"Hallelujah!" Olivia shouted. "Our very own Citizen Smith is going to start the revolution. He takes out a banker, raises the Red Flag above Downing Street and Hey Presto! - we have a dictatorship of the proletariat."

"But Olivia," said Henning, "you're ignoring the lessons of history. The Peasants' Revolt - led by Wat Tyler. *One man.*"

"And we all know what happened to him," Olivia replied. "They stuck his head on a spike if I remember right."

"Tracey, you're not saying much," said Henning. "And you've got the most to lose. What's your view on direct action?"

"I don't know," she replied, looking bewildered. "You and Paul .... you seem so sure of yourselves... all this stuff about firing squads. To be honest I've got enough on my plate just paying the bills."

Henning and Paul exchanged condescending glances. Tracey looked at Henning and then turned to Olivia.

"I don't see where you're coming from," she told her. "You say we've got to work harder and tighten our belts. That's OK for people like you with money behind them."

33

"People like you … with money behind them," exclaimed Henning. "Those are the words I've been waiting for Tracey. Bravo!"

Reports are coming in of a security alert outside Downing Street. Two plain clothes officers guarding the Secretary of State for Work and Pensions have sustained minor knife wounds. Their injuries are not thought to be serious.

"Matthew - glad you could make it. Can I introduce you to Detective Inspector Cooper of the Anti-Terrorism Branch?"

The Vice Chancellor slowly poured coffee for both men. Henning saw that the old man's hands were shaking.

"Matthew," he continued, "let me bring you up to speed on that unfortunate business yesterday. Looks like it's one of your part-timers."

"We have the suspect down at the station," added the Inspector sternly. "Not making much sense … just rambling on about Marx and Lenin."

"Christ – it's Paul, isn't it?" Henning said. "I knew he was a bit zealous but I didn't think he'd go that far. Such a bright boy. What a waste."

"Did you say *Paul?*" asked the Vice Chancellor. "Matthew, the attack was carried out by a female… er, Tracey Grimshaw. Have I got that right, Inspector?"

"Yes, Vice Chancellor," he replied. "The only suspect as far as we know. She lives in a flat in Whitechapel. No previous history of violence, but used to get a regular pasting from her ex. Usual story: claiming benefits and in debt up to her eyeballs. Social services have taken the brat into care."

"Inspector," said Henning, "I'm finding this a bit much to take in. In class Miss Grimshaw - Tracey - never had much to say. No strong opinions… quiet as a mouse."

"Well, your mouse certainly roared yesterday," said the Vice Chancellor.

"Was there any evidence of a conspiracy?" asked Henning.

"No - none at all," replied the Inspector. "In fact it's down to a tip-off from one your students that we got to her before she reached the Minister. She told us that she was worried about the political direction the class was taking."

"And what about Tracey?" asked Henning.

"She was very agitated...and confused. One minute she was blubbing on about her son, then she was spouting some nonsense about the personal as political."

Henning lowered his eyes.

"But the Chief reckons she's more psychiatric than forensic."

"So it's a medical matter, then?" added the Vice Chancellor with obvious relief.

"That's what it seems like," replied the officer.

"So, Matthew, it looks like the Faculty is in the clear," the Vice Chancellor concluded warmly.

"But what about the part-timers?" asked Henning.

"Well, there are no teaching staff available for them, but young Paul has offered to step into the breach. Unpaid of course."

"What about me?" asked Henning.

"Don't worry, Matthew - you'll keep the pension, but your retirement starts today. See that your desk is cleared by five. It's just market forces old chap. *Nothing personal*."

Where Have All The Cowboys Gone?

WAYNE HARDMAN

When I was looking through the local cinema listings recently I couldn't help asking: where have all the cowboys gone?

I still remember those Saturday afternoon matinees at our local cinema when there was always a serial showing Flash Gordon, Zorro or Superman. But the main feature film would have been a cowboy movie: not Butch Cassidy and the Sundance Kid but the good old boys like Tom Mix, Tex Ritter, Randolph Scott, Lash LaRue or even Gene Autry – the singing cowboy. These were followed by Roy Rogers and his partner Dale Evans, The Lone Ranger and Tonto, Hopalong Cassidy, the Cisco Kid or Smiley Burnett.

There were lots more, too and Tom Mix started it all. He was only a name to me but my Dad told me about him. Mix was the first American Cowboy – he'd started as a rodeo rider in the 1920s, progressed through the circus as a rider and horse stuntman and he paved the way for all the others when he became the first Western movie stuntman-actor. Everyone in America knew who Mix was by the late 20s: he made over 400 films and a fifteen episode serial in the 1930s. They were mostly silent films and, sadly, all but a handful have been destroyed by the elements or poor storage – a familiar story in early Hollywood.

What made Tom unique? He was the real McCoy: an accomplished rodeo star who could ride, do trick riding, roping, take on the bad guys and woo the ladies. All his rodeo and circus training paid off handsomely. When the average man's wage was less than half a dollar a day this Hollywood cowboy earned around $17,000 a week during the peak of his career in the late 30s. He did it the hard way, sustaining more than eighty serious injuries in a career where he always did his own film stunts. Ex-Marshall Wyatt Earp was a friend who acted as an advisor on Mix's films.

He was born in Pennsylvania but moved out West to become a cowboy years before he became King of the Cowboys. Even when Roy Rogers took over that title there were comic books featuring Tom Mix ten years after he died in a road accident in the Arizona desert.

Gene Autry was the next Western hero and when they heard him sing he was advised to get into show business. It was good advice: Autry turned a $5 mail order guitar into a career as Hollywood's original singing cowboy, appearing on radio, TV and the movie screen.

His talent for performing made his fortune. In those days you could tell the good guys from the baddies by the colour of their hat. Gene wore the white hat – always the hero, with his horse, Champion and a song that needed to be sung. He first sang on radio in 1928, and then went on to films and the lead role in television's "Gene Autry Show" from 1950 to 1956. He made 95 movies in all and is still the only Western star on the list of all-time box office money makers. He released 635 records during his career and co-wrote his trademark tune – "Back In The Saddle Again" – and was awarded gold records for such favourites as "Rudolph the Red-Nosed Reindeer", "Here Comes Santa Claus", "Peter Cottontail" and "You Are My Sunshine".

In 1956 Gene got off Champion and hung up his spurs. By then he owned four radio stations, a hotel in Palm Springs and many other properties. In 1982 he sold his Los Angeles TV station KTA for $245 million and was the majority owner of the L.A Angels baseball team. For many years he was on the Forbes magazine list of the 400 wealthiest Americans. And it all started with a song.

The Gene Autry Western Heritage Museum was opened in 1988 to honour the kind of cowboys he played onscreen. Among the items in the $54 million museum is a 1870s-era steam fire engine from Nevada, guns owned by Annie Oakley and Wyatt Earp and costumes of TV's Lone Ranger and Tonto. Friends who came for the dedication in Los Angeles' Griffith Park reflected on the influence of their one-time matinee idol.

"My older brothers used to take me to the shows to see Gene Autry and Roy Rogers," said musician Glen Campbell.

Dale Evans and Roy Rogers recalled Autry as one of their peers. "It was an era," said Evans. "Westerns were it."

"Gene said he'd have liked to make a true Western," recalled actor Buddy Ebsen. "He said his were a kind of fantasy… so you couldn't really believe them – but you could be entertained by them."

In 1991 a letter written about Gene Autry in the 1930s by film producer Al Levoy was found in the Republic Pictures archive. It said that Autry had no future in Hollywood. Autry's response: "A lot of that is true. I got better as I went along. I couldn't get any worse."

You might not recall Leonard Slye but most people have heard of Roy Rogers – the name Slye chose to work in the movies. Roy became the next "King of the Cowboys" during his long career as a folksy singing hero of TV and movies. In 1937 he signed for Republic Pictures, replacing their departing star Gene Autry. He starred in more than eighty Westerns and often co-starred with cowgirl Dale Evans who he married in 1947.

Rogers's famous horse – Trigger – was a Palomino stallion with a flowing white mane that became a favourite with Rogers's fans. In the 1950s he moved into TV with his own "Roy Rogers Show." His theme song, which he sang with Dale Evans, was the gentle, cheery "Happy Trails To You".

When Trigger died, Roy had him stuffed and mounted and put on display at the Roy Rogers Museum in Victorville, California.

After Roy Rogers came Clayton Moore and Jay Silverheels playing The Lone Ranger and Tonto on TV and in films that had an expensive look, being filmed in beautiful colour with excellent sound, a solid cast of familiar faces and a very good musical score, including the thrilling *William Tell Overture* that introduces the Lone Ranger riding his horse, Silver, on a rugged Western landscape.

The action scenes allowed the actors to display their fine horsemanship, with daring rescues and the various disguises used by the Masked Man to track down the outlaws against the grand mountain vistas of southern Utah. These provided the backdrop for the Lone Ranger and his Indian sidekick as they rode the trails for justice to bring peace to a young territory that was hoping for statehood. Their horses helped them fend off arrows or bullets and you could rely on Silver to race off to get the Sherriff, the Rangers or cavalry whenever his master needed their help, and to jump that gap in the gorge when the following bad guys couldn't.

Whatever happened to those carefree days of hope, trust and good guys that wore white hats? Why is nobody making cowboy films any more? Have we lost our sense of simple adventure? Are we now too cynical to believe that there are only good guys and bad guys and nothing in between? They say that crime doesn't pay. Tell that to the bankers and policy makers and see a smile creep over their faces.

Bring back the cowboys in white hats: they'll sort them out like they did in the old days.

Revenge Is Fattening

CAIT VALLELY

1977.

Love enticed Amaya to Madrid. Lack of it made her want to leave. She longed to be in her father's country house in the cool of San Sebastian. However, Paco said a wife's place was by her husband's side, which was next to impossible, as he was never at home. His time was spent with his fellow civil guards, talking about the good old days when General Franco was alive. So here she was with her daughter, on a sticky September Sunday waiting for Carmen, her sister-in-law.

Carmen's dingy flat, boxed in on the sixth row of a brick and mortar honeycomb, was an oven. Months of sunshine had steeped it in heat. At six that morning, Carmen had thrown open the windows and rolled up the blinds. Beams of light hit and ran from the mingy furniture. The rays danced around the chubby table, dressed in a chunky cracked oilcloth falling in stiff folds to the worn, well-washed floor. The sun then skipped to a spongy sofa squashed against the wall. On the opposite side a crockery cabinet, fattened by coats of paint and varnish, gobbled up the rest of the space. The family of five spent their days squeezed into this room. Carmen, who had been cooking all morning, shouted from the narrow kitchen.

"Pedro, make sure you put the Nivea cream in the bag - we don't want the kids sunburned like last week. Come on, hombre, get those bottles of water down to the car - it's after eight. Do you want us to be stuck in traffic like last Sunday?"

All Madrid could be illuminated with the voltage of happiness the family emitted. Another Sunday of fresh air and open spaces. The kids free of the straitjacket of city dwelling would run wild through the grass and swim in the cool river. Carmen buzzed with impatience. She wanted to be on the riverbank, scouting a site shaded by the scarce trees that stood proudly in the sought-after sandy patches. Around these the Madridlenos set up house. Portable cookers, deck chairs, packs of cards and thousands of odds and ends poured out of the Seat 600 cars.

"Pedro we have to go to Calle Velazquez to pick up 'The Basque' at half past eight." Her mouth screeched to a halt and the air filled with dense anger. "Half past eight! That fat pig is going to keep us from getting a good spot. That fancy apartment her father had bought them as a wedding present was better than any shotgun in getting Paco to marry that fool of a woman. The lazy cow has put on at least twenty kilos."

Amaya, the Basque, and her daughter Francisca were crammed into the back of the car along with the kids. At the river, Carmen spied the bright daisies of her eldest's sister sunshade and started to leap up and down yelling at her sibling. She flung some towels over her shoulder and dragged two baskets full of food from the boot. After plonking two enormous watermelons on Amaya's lap, who was still trying to manoeuvre her way out of the tiny car, she ordered Pedro to carry the rest of the stuff. It didn't take her long to plough her way to the bit of parched grass, shaded by the gaudy umbrella, where she dropped her heavy load and wrapped her arms around her sister. The rest followed with the kissing and hugging greeting. As they finished, the younger sister arrived and they got into the full swing of the embracing act again. Little Francisca was swung from sister to sister in a frenzy of loud smacking kissing and screeches of, "Ay, look how beautiful she is: the image of Paco."

They ignored Amaya, so she edged away to stand by two coolboxes, which seemed to be the border of their space. However, hostile looks from the neighbouring family made her realize she was on the wrong side of the frontier. Stepping over the portable fridges to get back to their picnic area, she hunched down and slouched to a vacant spot. Rooting in the pocket of her loose tent size dress she dug out a paperback, *The Mirror Cracked...* by Agatha Christie, and stuck her head into it. The peace she'd hoped for didn't come dropping slow. Instead, prickly legs started to crawl up her lower back. Jumping up in fright, she used Agatha Christie to swat hysterically at the creepy insect but the book walloped the daylights out of a man's hairy back, which ended up redder than an English tourist in Benidorm, but not as red as Amaya. Shamefaced, she fled to the water and hid herself in it.

The dive into the river stirred up murky memories of her life with Paco. Young, romantic, Amaya thought she'd follow her handsome husband

41

anywhere and not look back. However, living in a pale quavering light of little love gives a rosy glow to the past. The weak flame of their love was quenched the day she lost her unborn son. Amaya was well used to the pushing and insults, but her baby couldn't take it: he left her body. When she was emptied of her child, she was emptied of love, too. The nothingness was unbearable, so she filled it with hatred. She went to sleep repeating the litanies of hurts Paco had done her. While she slept, wrath dripped through the slats of her soul, festering into stinking manure. A filthy rage woke her in the morning and shoved her out of bed. Her every pore oozed loathing, helping her feel, to be alive. But it was hungry, opening its mouth, howling to be fed. To quieten it, she stuffed it with every scrap of food she could lay her hands on. The weight piled on. Her outer body began to reflect the ugliness within. The hideous shield of lard gave Paco more ammunition with which to rebuke her.

"You big fat heap. You're so lucky there's no divorce in this country. God help me, I'm stuck with you. No one would put up with a stupid pig like you, not even the ignorant Basques. You'd disgust them like you disgust me, swine".

Amaya ate more and more, but food wasn't what the hatred wanted. She discovered it was Paco's blood it screamed for. Amaya and Francisca had been baking when Paco came into the kitchen. He growled at her to stop speaking in Basque - he didn't want any child of his listening to the language of ETA terrorists. Amaya tried to explain that most Basque families spoke Basque at home; it was more natural for them than to speak in Castilian. She added it wouldn't do Francisca any harm to be bilingual. The slap she got across the face didn't hurt as much as when he said, "When are you going to get it into your stupid head that Spain is one country with one official language? Thank God you lost that boy. You would have taught him that language of terrorists behind my back. His Excellency was right to forbid its use. Let this be the last time I hear you speaking it in my house."

Next thing Amaya knew she was stabbing her husband in the chest over and over and screaming that he would soon be with that hateful dictator, Generalissimo Franco. Paco caught hold of her arm and forced her fist open. The weapon fell to the ground with a dull thud. Surprised at the

42

sound, she looked down and saw a wooden spoon. In her blind rage she had grabbed a spoon instead of the carving knife. Her free hand reached for the sharp blade but the terrified screams of Francisca stopped her. The chocolate eyes of her daughter were melting in horror. Amaya bent to pick her up but she ran and clung fearfully to her Papa's legs.

"Goaaaaaal." Pedro shouting at the top of his voice jerked her back to the present. Carmen's husband, hidden among the reeds had the transistor stuck to his ear, was listening to the Real Madrid game. It took him a while to recognize the slim figured woman as his sister–in–law. Amaya nodded to Pedro letting him know his secret was safe with her. The sack of a dress was slipped over her wet togs and she made her way back to the camp. Paco had arrived and was holding Francisca. When the little girl saw Amaya, she wiggled out of her father's arms and ran to her mother. "Who needs hatred when you could have a bundle of joy wrapping their tiny arms around your neck?" Amaya thought.

It hadn't been easy to destroy the darkness clinging onto her soul. She didn't want to repeat the magic words that Basque children learned from their mothers to cope with the tribulations of life. The first time she said the aspiration it felt like a chisel cutting chunks out of her insides. The encrusted resentment loosened with each saying. Hardened flakes of anger turned to soft leaves that rose and scattered as though the prayer was a car driving by. Twirling gently in the breeze they spelt "divorce" as she whispered once more, "Thy Will Be Done." Peace and indifference replaced the anger. She could give Paco a happy smile without any effort - it was wasted on him. He and his brothers-in-law were condemning the legalisation of the Communist Party in April. They were going to do something so Francisco Franco wouldn't be turning in his grave. Amaya picked up her book. She liked the changes in Spain. Just like her it would continue to grow in a different way and be a better place.

In 1981 divorce was legalized in Spain.

In October 1982 there was a failed Coup d 'Etat by the civil guards.

Tempo '64

FRANKIE McPHILLIPS

Best to Charlton... to Law... back to Crerand... back to Best. He beats one man, two men - he shoots. Goal. Goal - Manchester United 2 Tottenham Hotspur 0. Best salutes the Stretford End and turns punching the air. A shrill whistle sounds and a roar of "Woods" sends the players scattering, Best and Law straight through the Stretford end and into Armstrong's coal yard; Charlton and Greaves jump over into Mrs Brady's garden. Crerand and Harry Gregg, the bravest, head straight up The Diamond, quickly rubbing the sweat from their flushed faces and round Armstrong's corner to meet the constable face to face. A mannerly salute and a "Good day, constable."

"Good afternoon, girls," he replies with a wry, knowing smile as he travels past. After a few yards the boys turn and watch as the big-framed constable pedals his small bicycle down the main street, its frame straining under his great frame and weight, legs set out at crazy angles like a circus clown. Past the Stretford End he travels and further up the street leans the bike against his home wall. One hour for lunch. Great joy - and play can resume at Old Trafford immediately.

In the heat of the sun the playing surface would sometimes deteriorate, with bubbles of black tar covering the road. The chips thrown over this by the council made underground conditions even more treacherous, but these were minor deterrents as we played out our FA Cup Finals and Internationals. The rules were simple: the ball was rolled down The Diamond gradient and was centred or returned back up hill from just short of Kidney's hotel window. Right footed "centerers" had an advantage here and we met the centred balls with flying feet or heads, aiming our efforts at Armstrong's coal yard door.

Three goals and you're in was the rule as we battled for possession. "Lorry," roared the lookout as our other main interrupter of games turned The Diamond, gears straining noisily to reduce speed on the steep slope, heading for Crieve quarry and a new load of gravel.

"Tea's ready," came the shout from my sister, and the shout nearly always had to be repeated before I would withdraw reluctantly from the game. Food was gulped down before a hasty return to Old Trafford.

Although Old Trafford was the main arena different sporting grounds could easily be frequented on the same day. In through the Stretford End nets and through Armstrong's sliding coal yard door was the Oval, Kennington. Here fiery Freddie Trueman, the fastest bowler by far in Tempo, launched hard sponge balls at tomato box wickets to cries of "Howzat," "LBW," "Four," "Six," and "Oh my bloody shin!" As the tomato boxes gradually disintegrated under fiery Freddie's onslaught oil drums were substituted.

The rules came straight from Lords. Rule 1: ball hit straight out over Armstrong's three storey house - 6 runs. Rule 2: into Armstrong's garden - 4 runs. Rule 3: sliced to the left and Primrose Kidney's garden meant lost ball with little chance of getting back.

Other rules were a bit more complicated: ball caught off any roof - you're out. Ball landing on timber yard planks - you're out. Ball landing in large coal scuttle - you're out.

When fiery Freddie's bowling was on song the wicket keeper was in as much danger as the batsman. He was allowed the safer option of standing on a box behind an open window three yards behind the wicket where he had two choices: 1. Try and catch the ball or 2. Duck for dear life.

In the summer, when the hay was rucked, Kennington Oval moved a mile out the Brookeborough road to Callaghan's hay meadow. Here proper wickets with stumps cut from the surrounding ditches were set up. Charlton, Best, Law, Greaves, Sandro Mazzola and the rest, directed to their proper fielding places by fiery Freddie, would have to adopt their skills of batting and bowling to the wider spaces whilst trying to avoid running into haystacks. Games were never restricted by overs or time. No light - not bad light - stopped play as the late evening mists rose over the mown hayfields of Lissnabann and Carnaguiltagh. We traipsed home tired, our sweaty bodies sometimes cooled by a soft summer breeze and our way often lighted by a rising Eucharistic moon over Coonian.

In poorer weather Old Trafford and The Oval would sometimes be abandoned and this restriction of our first love - the outdoors - led us indoors to marvel at television. By 1964 there were at least four televisions in the village with different viewing options. Armstrong's could only be viewed from the outside, sitting on the windowsill, looking at a small flickering screen at the far end of the sitting room. This was less than satisfactory but some of the Manchester United squad and Geronimo sat there anyway and gazed in, until Mrs Armstrong came rapping the window sharply and closed the curtains with a flourish.

Across the street, past Nixon's Butchers, Kitty Gallagher had TV No. 2 and the best selection of sweets in town. We crowded in for *Love Hearts, Liquorice Allsorts,* sherbet filled melt-in–your-mouth-saucers and McGowan's stick-to-your-teeth toffee. Some good Catholic boys off sweets - but not stealing - for Lent would continue to pilfer and on Easter Sunday enjoy the vast accumulated wealth of their crimes. Kitty was selective in her choice of viewer and she only allowed some of us, in small groups, to watch the telly.

No such restriction across the road at the TV capital of Tempo: Campbell's front room. Here, in a small dark room, sat almost all of Tempo's under ten population plus some older boys. Backsides on ground at front, seating section a ring of armchairs midway down the room and standing room only at the back. Mrs Campbell - who already had a large family of her own - didn't seem to mind the crush as she lit the small log fire with petrol-covered logs. As the flames whooshed up the chimney silence was called for as flying arrows zipped through the air and thudded into English oak: the first strains of *Robin Hood, Robin Hood riding through the glen* settled us down for the evening's entertainment.

From the western plains to the Black Hills of Dakota, from Sherwood Forest to the treasured islands of the South Pacific, from Fagin's Den to the Admiral Benbow, TV in Campbell's front room introduced us to a world of wonder and adventure. Sir Lancelot and Robin Hood, Cheyenne and Bronco Lane fired our imaginations as reflections of their swordfights and gunfights flickered round a room full of silent, transfixed faces.

We soaked it all up, took it all in and acted out our own adventures of Long John Silver and Huckleberry Finn. We paddled oil drum rafts down the great Mississippi and landed on a sandy treasure island just this side of the barbed wire sewer pipe below Tempo bridge. For these adventures,

46

and Cowboys and Indians battles, the Manchester United and the MCC first eleven squads were joined by other players who didn't play cricket or football but excelled in other areas.

Sitting Bull and Geronimo couldn't kick back doors or snow off a rope but they could creep silently on their bellies for hundreds of yards through leafy undergrowth, and pick out the cavalry at Fort Apache, cutting their throats with rubber knives. Or they would pick them off with bow-shot arrows made of the finest Langham plantation sally. Geronimo was particularly fearless: he would cross the barbed wire sewer pipe above the Rio Grande, even in flood, or jump into the water with his clothes on and do almost every dare and double dare requested of him. Sometimes the same posse who gave the great Indian chief feats of valour to perform in return for his freedom would break recently smoked pipes of peace and turn and hunt him like a dog. He could be tied to a tree and left to die in the midday sun or made to walk a plank over a Rio Grande turn hole.

Cowboy battles could be along the whole plantation as we crept up the length of the Colorado, past the RUC barracks and right up to Langham's Manor. Extreme silence and Indian stealth here or the gamekeeper and dogs would add some unwanted reality to our adventure.

The great United team of the Sixties and the Indian tribes of the Great Plains all had their day. Great Players retired gracefully, or went to Macclesfield Town and the Isthmian League. The Cowboys and Indians of the Langham plantation drifted away and rarely ventured back to the scenes of their great victories, their forts and leafy hut hideaways grown over; their skills of whittling bow, arrow and spear, and building rafts and moss-floored huts of beech and sycamore were not passed on to new adventurers. Old Trafford on The Diamond remained open as football retained its interest 'though some players were now spending more time at McBarron's corner where leather-covered transistor radios blared out the new music of the Fab Four and Dylan. The times they were a-changing. Igor Chislenko, the great Russian World Cup hero, had burst on The Diamond football scene roaring his name. After a lot of huffing and puffing he ran out of steam fairly quickly, and Brylcreem, tight trousers and the Swinging Blue Jeans brought a swift end to his playing career. Fiery Freddie Trueman went on to coach cricket on the manicured lawns of

Upper Malone and the rest of the England Test team that won the ashes at Rosie Grey's turned to football and played together for years to come.

Nearly ten years later I was walking from Charing Cross tube station to the main line station above. It was late and I had just passed the almost permanent cardboard village of the homeless, when I swore I heard a voice calling, "McPhillips!"

I walked on slightly startled, and then I heard it again, this time more clearly. I turned to see four tall figures walking from the shadows under the bridge. As they came nearer in the dark I began to recognise the figure of one of them. It was Geronimo - the fearless hero of many an attack on Fort Apache but looking as fearful as his namesake now, standing over six foot tall in spotted bandana.

"Hello, Tom," I said. He shook my hand, asked me what I was doing in London and told me if I was ever stuck for a place to stay I could come up to Islington and stay with him.

I thanked him for his offer and just before we parted company one of his friends showed me a clenched fist adorned with a bicycle chain. "Someone's going to get it tonight," he said.

Geronimo was now in charge of his own posse: no longer the hunted but now the hunter. As I watched them enter a nearby tunnel I shuddered at the thought of their next encounter and was glad that I had never made him walk the plank at McCarron's Turnhole on the mighty Rio Grande.

Missing Rose

DIANE JARDEL

Private Detective Mervin Goldsmith walked round the room, looking for information about the woman who had disappeared. "The police have already found that she didn't take a bus or plane?"

"Yes, that's why I called you," said Maureen, the missing woman's daughter.

"Right, I need to find out what..." he looked down at his notes, "your mother Rose was doing before she disappeared. I need you to get her handbag and log into her laptop."

Whilst Maureen followed his instructions, the detective looked around the dining room.

"Are these her children?" he asked the missing woman's husband, looking at three photos on the wall of a boy and two girls dressed in graduation outfits.

"Yes," her husband grunted as if to say, are you stupid or what? He hated the stranger's intrusion into his home and into his life.

The detective scanned the other walls and saw a drawing of a lake with palm trees around it.

"Ah, the handbag," he said as he sat down at the dining room table, flexed his fingers and pulled open the zip. "And the wallet".

The black wallet bulged full of receipts and coins. Inside it there was a photo of a young man: on the back was written: Dorian Gribbon, B Sc Hons. Chemistry. And there were two photos of a girl with flashing brown eyes.

"That's my brother and sister," Maureen explained.

"It's OK. You don't have to explain anything. Just let me get my bearings," said the detective. "Why would she leave her wallet behind?"

The first receipt he found was for Gordon's Chemist Toddler Wipes. He picked up the second receipt and read out, "Film House

Enniskillen…30/04/2011 at 18.34. Two 3D glasses and two seats for the Film *Thor* at £13.00 on her Visa Debit card. Hmm."

The detective looked through the pockets of the wallet for the Boots Advantage card and her debit card but didn't find them. "She's taken them," he said. He found a scrap of folded paper. Several notes were written on it: *You arrive at 16.50* and a drawing of a bird with the words *But I'm not used to it* written on its belly. The name *Erik Erikson* was written at a different angle and underneath *I am trying to be good but I'm not used to it*. He opened up the piece of paper and found two flower petals that had been pressed between the folds. "Tulip petals, I think." Then on a smaller scrap of paper *Primo Levi – Is this a man?* A shopping list: *dried mushrooms, Ryvitas, basil, toms, red onion, sweet corn cob, sweet potato, courgettes, avocados, baby lettuce, 3 aubergines, 2 apples, frozen corn on the cob and pumpkin*. And a card with the name *Rose* written in a way he didn't recognise.

"That's Japanese script," Maureen explained. "She had a friend in Scotland who wrote the meaning of her name in Japanese. She treasures it because the girl took her own life when she returned home to Japan."

"Can't you leave my wife's things alone?" said the husband, fingers embedded in two fists, blood pressure rising.

"Daddy, he's just trying to find out more, so we can have some idea of why she's disappeared. Leave it to me - I'll sort it out."

"I don't know why you had to bring this detective in," he muttered, and left the room.

"Well, what do I know so far about your mum? She likes going to 3-D cinema screenings…she's addicted to fruit and veg…and she bought sushi in Stansted Airport."

There was no response from Maureen. Why was he so flippant at such a frightening time for her?

"Ah, her blog address. Where's the computer?"

"She even left her mobile behind," said Maureen. "She usually texts me every day and she's got a terrible memory for numbers."

As the detective looked through her blog and the history of her searches, Rose was wandering around Bundoran. She had been walking along a

50

country lane, going home from her daughter's house when she blacked out and sunk down onto the grass verge. When she awoke she thought she had just sat down for a moment. Then she stood up slowly and walked towards the main road. While she waited to cross a man drove up in a truck behind her. She couldn't tell which way he would be turning. If he turned left she could cross the road without waiting for him.

"Are you turning this way?" she shouted, pointing right and mouthing each word clearly so he could read her lips.

He opened his window. "Will you be wanting a lift?" he asked.

"No, no," she laughed, "I just want to cross the road."

She couldn't remember why she had to cross the road or where she was going: it was all a blank but she loved the idea of doing something spontaneously.

"Oh, hold on, yes – I'll take a ride."

"Where will you be going to?"

"The sea," she answered. She liked the sea.

"What's your name?" the driver asked when they arrived at the next village.

"What's my name?" she thought.

She looked down at a newspaper on the seat next to her, and saw a report with the name "Kathleen" written in bold letters.

"Kathleen," she told him.

The driver looked puzzled and nodded.

She enjoyed the wind rushing through her hair, watching the rolling hills and lonely birds hovering over the brilliant green meadows on one side and the tranquil lough to her right.

"Why can't I remember my name?" she thought as she looked down at her red raincoat and denim jeans. She caught sight of her image in the mirror: a woman with brown hair and a round face. She didn't recognise her but felt content sitting in the van travelling to the sea.

"Here we are," said the driver, "Bundoran sea front."

She got out of the truck and waved goodbye to the driver as he set off again. She wandered down to the shore, letting the water lap against her feet as she held her sandals in her hands and felt a kind of freedom.

As dusk fell she found a bus shelter and sat down; her eyelids started drooping and she lay on her side and fell asleep. A barking dog woke her. She felt quite dizzy as she stood up, stretched and wandered towards a café and found a toilet. Looking at an unfamiliar face in the mirror she washed her hands, dried them on some toilet paper and went into the café to buy a drink.

She smiled at the woman behind the counter. "A cup of tea please."

"Now then," said the woman, "that will be two euros."

"Oh yes, money," stammered Rose.

The café owner studied Rose's face: she looked quite vacant and was having trouble focusing.

"Have you got your handbag?" the woman asked.

Rose looked around. "Oh, no."

"Look in your raincoat pocket. Have you got a purse in there?"

Rose fumbled and found a blue fabric purse.

"Oh, I found it," she announced, beaming. She ignored the debit card and took out two pounds.

"Enjoy your tea," said the woman, who assumed that Rose was just a bit slow.

After her tea Rose walked back to the shore. It was a warm day and she sat near a man and woman building a sandcastle with three children on the beach. The youngest child toddled towards her and showed her a pebble.

"Pebble," she said and opened her hand for it. The baby put it in her hand then opened his hand.

"Pebble me," he insisted, and she gave the pebble back to him.

The detective was checking out the missing woman's laptop, and clicked on the History icon.

"Jesus, does she spend all day on the computer? She's carried out twelve different searches. And look on her email site – she's got about fifty messages from LinkedIn...writing groups in Canada...South Africa and Mexico. How does she cope?"

"I don't know," sobbed Maureen.

"This note," he said, holding it up. "Why would she draw a bird? Let's see who she phoned last."

Maureen punched 1471 into the land phone.

"It's my Auntie's number."

The detective phoned the missing woman's sister.

"Oh, what's happened?" she asked. After she had been told, she explained the jottings.

"Rose is writing about her life and I found a letter she wrote to our mum when she was six. She was staying with our aunt and was finding it difficult to talk to her so she wrote things down.

I'm trying to be good but I'm not used to it – what does that mean?" the detective asked.

"It was a difficult time for her," said the sister. "Maybe writing about it will help her emotionally."

"Thank you."

"Tell me as soon as you hear from her, won't you?"

"Yes, yes."

In Bundoran, Rose had started chatting to the parents of the children, commenting on the children's play.

"She's fascinated with that shell. Isn't it wonderful seeing children discover the world?"

"Where are you from?" asked the children's mother.

"Um….I don't know," said Rose and started crying. "I can't remember my name either."

"Let's look in your pockets…a purse. What's in it?"

"Some money and a debit card," said Rose as she looked through its contents.

"There you are. Your name is Rose…Rose M. Gribbon."

The name meant nothing to her. Had she stolen the card?

"Oh what shall I do?" she asked.

"Come on - let's go to our hotel and look you up on the internet," the father said.

Rose felt shaky. "I'm frightened….I don't know who I am or where I come from. I might remember in a few minutes and you won't have to look at my bank details."

The father shrugged his shoulders. "I was only trying to help."

"Thank you. It was good chatting to you."

Rose stood up, brushed the sand from her jeans and wandered away. She felt her heart beating quickly and tried to control it by taking slow, deep breaths. She wasn't ready to discover who she was. What if she had run away from a bad relationship, or if she was in trouble with the police? What if she didn't remember her family? Could she cope living with strangers?

She walked up to Main Street and went into the Holyrood Hotel to use the phone but it didn't accept sterling coins. She walked back into the street and saw a taxi parked there.

"Can you take me to the nearest hospital?" she asked the taxi driver.

"The Sheil Hospital is in Ballyshannon. Will I be taking you there?" he asked.

"Yes, please," she said, trying to sound confident.

She got into the taxi and tried not to panic as they drove to Ballyshannon.

"Now, here's the hospital," the driver pointed.   "That'll be five euros."

"I haven't got any euros," she said, her voice trembling. "I've lost my memory and I have to see a doctor."

"I'll take pounds, then," he told her.

She walked into the Accident and Emergency Department. "I think I've got concussion," she told a clerk at the reception desk. "I've lost…I've lost my memory."

"Sit yourself down there," the receptionist pointed to the seats in the waiting room to her left. "I'll call you when a doctor is free."

Rose sat next to a woman who was hugging a little boy. His left eye was bruised and swollen.

"I've been sitting here for an hour waiting to see the doctor.   I wish they'd hurry up."

"I know exactly what you mean. When I took my son to…to hospital in Enniskillen…I can remember!" she shouted as she stood up, attracting the

54

attention of everyone waiting for the doctor. She didn't care if they thought she was mad.

"Have you got a phone book?" she asked the receptionist.

"No but you can call the operator on this phone."

Her hands shook as she held the phone and asked for the number of Mrs Rose M. Gribbon.

"You're through," the operator told her.

"Yes, I am through," she thought.

Marathon Romance

SEAMUS CAROLAN

I had flirted with her over the years but the response had been a mixture of annoyance, contempt and pity. Fun runs, five and ten kilometre sponsored charity runs didn't even merit the flicker of an eye-lid. Twenty-six point two miles non-stop or sit in your armchair seemed to be the message if I was to achieve this particular item from my list of "Things to do before I die" drawn up on my big five zero birthday.

However desirable the achievement, or admirable the aspiration, a person will not even attempt a task until ready for it. In the spring of 1998, when *Help the Aged* came calling for fundraisers to run the New York Marathon, I was ready, and sufficiently unaware of the difficulty of the task to agree to participate.

Miss Marathon is an alluring but demanding suitor who must be courted patiently, persistently and intensively if one is to have any chance of the finishing-line embrace on the allocated day. She completely ignored me at the start of my six month courtship when, fifty two years old, fourteen stone heavy and more or less completely unfit, I announced my intention to my wife and family and headed to Spring Grove Forest to commence training – at 7a.m. so no-one would see me. The first hundred yards or so was great – the cool April wind on my face – *Start Spreading the News, I'm leaving today* … humming in my brain. Then the legs began to complain bitterly and the sharply increased demand for oxygen sent my cardiovascular system into overdrive with red lights flashing vigorously, forcing me to a complete halt. Take it easy Seamus - walk a bit and get your second wind. You don't have to do this – it is voluntary, after all.

I covered a mile and a bit, mostly walking, that first morning and without some positive feedback from Lady Marathon I would have had to abandon my efforts: between that idea and this reality lay a terrible shadow of self-inflicted pain, dietary change and hours and hours of solitary running. I reflected anxiously on the chicken-and-egg aspect of needing to lose weight to be able to run, and needing to run in order to lose weight.

However, by the time I'd had a good shower, some nourishment, and settled in to my day job, I was warming to the idea. The journey of 26.2 miles can surely begin with a single tentative laboured mile. I could make a short phone call at any time, pull the pin, and that would be that.

Then disaster struck in the shape of two small news items placed by *Help the Aged* in the *Fermanagh Herald* and *Impartial Reporter* – informing all and sundry: *Roslea teacher to give Big Apple the run around.* There it was for all to see – students, parents, colleagues, family. I could either issue a denial or prepare to run.

My secret, optional exercise was immediately elevated to a first priority public must–be–completed project which required management: objectives, strategy, performance-indicators, task breakdown structures, dependency networks, monitoring, evaluation. The full project management package.

Maps with various lengths of runs, diet sheets, running schedules, rest schedules, warm up routines and warm down routines littered my study table. My poor unfortunate body became a machine which had to be completely re-jigged, adjusted, stretched and tightened to enable it to do things it didn't seem designed to do: work on a completely new fuel system, bereft of many of its traditional support mechanisms – morning fries, desserts, butter, salt, chocolate bars, fast food, days of inactivity. All changed. Utterly changed.

In fairness to Lady Marathon, she did give me the odd smile of encouragement and small rewards along the way. Running one, then two, then three, then seven miles non-stop, gave me confidence that this task was achievable. The stopping of the needle on the scales below thirteen, then twelve-and-a-half, and then the twelve stone mark; the completion of the ten mile Newry to Carlingford run, all drew from her indications that I was indeed becoming worthy of her attentions.

During the summer I explored the beautiful Slieve Beagh hills, running along every forest path and discovering a paradise of lakes and laneways of which I had been unaware: Jenkin, Cushkeery, Tawy, Asladee, Nabradagh, Shane Barnagh's Lake. The upland grasses, flowers, heather, berries, shrubs, birds, trees (even the forestry planted ones) created an idyllic environment in which to spend time jogging, which is probably a more accurate description of my activity than "running."

I reflected on the route my grandfather would have taken in the early years of the century, as he walked over these hills to hunts in the Clogher area. I revisited the turf banks at Mullaghfad where our family had cut and dried turf during the 1950s, and made a special pilgrimage to the ruins of the buildings on the farm once worked by the legendary poteen maker known as "The Guffin." Among many adventures were a nervous examination of the Cooneen ghost house, and a jog along Stramackilroy where, folklore has it, Shane Barnagh was done to death by Black Jemmy Hamilton on his way home to his hilltop fortress, still known as Shane Barnagh's Stables.

Sometime in early October, I trotted the twenty odd miles from my home out over Eshnadarragh to Eshawilligan, to Cooneen Chapel, past the Cooneen Ghost House, to Mullaghfad, through Dernahesco and Lannet, along the Long Hollow to Knockatallon Cross and home through Killmore and Derryheanlish, Deerpark, Lisnawesnagh and Roslea village. This was a pilgrimage to the roads of my boyhood years along which I had gone to fish, rob orchards, spread turf, drive cattle, walk to school and Mass, and cycle to dances: a gathering of all the memories and strengths of a rural upbringing; a revisiting of the places and experiences that had made me what I was, and which I would now need to draw upon to sustain me through the coming challenge.

On Staten Island we were marshalled, all 33,000 of us, at the approach to the Verrazano Bridge, on a beautiful sunny New York November morning. We were fuelled up on water and bananas and away we went, to bring six months hard labour to fruition. It was an unbelievable experience: Lady Marathon's promises were kept to the full, running across that long bridge through Brooklyn, Queens, The Bronx, Manhattan - places I had only dreamed of visiting and associated with all sorts of movies.

All along the route New Yorkers were out in strength applauding and shouting encouragement. My wife and daughter cheered me on in Brooklyn and Manhattan, but I was wilting badly as I got past twenty two miles when I entered Central Park. I was beyond my longest run and approaching the infamous "wall." After twenty three miles I was on autopilot, not running in Central Park, but following my father as we turned hay in a meadow in Tattymore, when I was a very small boy. Every now and then he would turn to me and smile saying, "Come on Seamus, you boy you. Come on Seamus, you boy you." And Seamus kept going, plodding all the weary way to the finish line and into the arms of two New York angels, one of whom put my finisher's medal around my neck while the other wrapped me in aluminium foil and helped me to a seat.

There I slumped – completely spent after my efforts. The rest of that day is a blur of congratulations by everyone, photos with other finishers from all over the world, memorable among whom were landmine victims from Vietnam. It felt great to have been there, completed the job and got the T-shirt. I could now cross "The Marathon" off my list.

Lady Marathon, however, is not so easily satisfied and beckons me irresistibly to embrace her again soon. Could she be thinking of....Beijing in November 2012?

The Skipper

IAN BUTLER

George was early today, walking speedily past the park to the night shelter, desperate to get into the warm. He was usually first in the queue and, even when he wasn't, those that knew him would stand aside to let him through to the front. The queue started about 4.30 pm every weekday, about half an hour before the shelter opened for the night. At weekends it was open all day, but during the week everyone had to go elsewhere. Most chose the church day centre, just up the river. George preferred to walk by himself.

On a good day he had a kind of dignity and was always scrupulous about his clothes and appearance. His face was like well worn leather which gave him the demeanour of a manual worker who had spent his working life outdoors. The younger homeless kids respected him because he had spent so much time on the road. On a bad day, however, George looked out of watery blood shot eyes with spidery capillary veins erupting across his face. On those days he walked with a bent, shuffling gait like a refugee broken by grief and loss.

In common with the other older hostel users he called his lifestyle, "Doing the Skipper." He couldn't tell anyone why: it was just the name for doing the rounds of night shelters and hostels. These places were a refuge, a respite when it got cold and they needed a warm, dry place to sleep.

Because the hostel was open only in the weekday evenings it made getting through the winter days very hard. This particular hostel gave care without the do-gooders poking their nose in. George liked that, the anonymity of it: no questions, no lies because, after all, he told himself the truth.

He had seen pretty much everything in these places and took pleasure in passing his knowledge on to others. He felt he knew all the different types of staff: the youngsters who would crack; the careerists; the do-gooders who always felt sorry for you right up to the point where you told them to leave you alone. George often thought they would be curtain twitchers at home, forever nosing into other people's business.

This night he bagged his favourite armchair and began his usual routine. The youngsters would get him a cup of tea and he would roll his fags, clasping the mug and allowing the heat to warm his fingers, even delighting in the prickling sensation that would announce his blood supply returning. When his fingers felt warm enough to put his tea down he began his nightly tobacco rolling. The tobacco was dry today as it was near the end of the packet, and George knew that he would have to roll them thin: they had to last till the next benefit cheque was delivered. He always told the young ones to stay away from ready made fags - they were an indulgence they couldn't afford. Despite his advice George always bought a pack of twenty Marlboro when he got his benefit because the smell and the feel of them made him remember happier times. He loved the smell of the packet opening for the first time and the neat order that the cigarettes were placed in. That first cigarette was absolute nectar - a treat after a few days living on dried up tobacco and whatever swoops he could get. Smoking that first cigarette made him feel important. It was one of his only times that he would look back, to when he had been in work and had a wife and kid. It would end the same way - a savage internal reproof – and he would return quickly to concentrate on whatever task that would take his mind away from the past.

The task was approached in the same way every day - always over a newspaper, to catch every little strand of tobacco, should any escape. A lot depended on how much he needed a drink. Sometimes he would shake very badly and he hated anyone to see this. For this reason he liked to make lots of smokes for his tin to get him through the times when the shakes prevented him rolling.

This night his hands were steady and the slow work of rolling began. Each fag would begin with the paper being smoothed on his knee and the tobacco being carefully laid on top. The further he got from his benefit money the less tobacco was placed there. He began rolling from the centre; the process ended with a lick of the gummed edge which sealed it all together.

George finished rolling his last cigarette and sat back and lit one. He took a gentle breath in and tasted the tobacco, letting it fill his lungs. It was harsh and bitter, yet ultimately fulfilling, a delight which George never failed to enjoy. Along with his tea it was the best thing that had happened that day.

He sat back and enjoyed his fag; his eyes felt heavy. He had walked by the river today and it had been bitterly cold. George realised that many of his days were the same, and since he had come out of prison only the geography had changed. It was nearly six now and in half an hour he would start to write to his son. It was always the same and he had long since run out of different ways to say "I am sorry," different ways of asking for his forgiveness. It was the pastor in the nick who had suggested that he wrote letters to his son Tom. The pastor said that he may be able to help himself and begin the process of "moving on". That hadn't happened and there was no moving on, but he still wrote the letters every day.

No one ever explained what "moving on" meant. Never told him where that would take him. Would it help him to forget? That was pointless: he knew he was responsible and must pay for it. The clock moved towards the time and George got out his bookies' pen and some paper. The staff knew that he mustn't be disturbed. They had learned from experience to leave him alone.

Dear Tom,

I had a good day today and I walked for ages. I saw the river at Richmond as I am staying near there. I would have loved to have taken you there to see the boats, and the bridges. It is a great sight and you would have loved it. Your Mum and I used to come here a lot when we were young, and we did some of our courting here. I would have loved to have got you a drink and held your hand as I walked you down the river bank. You know how much I love you and so did your Mum. She loved you so much Tom. I can't tell you what happened that night but I am sorry. Again and again I want to say sorry to you and to Mum. I was drinking that night and if I hadn't it might not have happened. I know that it is a pitiful excuse but at the time I couldn't see the harm.

Goodnight little man. I love you,

Daddy.

George would always sit quietly after writing his letter and today was no different. He pondered what he had written and asked for a cup of tea. He knew that his mate would ask him soon for a game of crib and he would snap out of it. His mate, Danny, was an Irish guy who got left behind when his family went home. He couldn't persuade his missus that he would give up the drink. Danny had a lovely set of expressions that made George smile. He would say "he was giving off" instead of "losing his rag" but George's favourite was when Danny wanted some quiet: he would say "Give my head peace." It made him laugh the first time he heard it and it never failed to make him smile whenever Danny used it.

Danny invited him to play crib and George accepted, sitting at the dining table which was the largest piece of furniture in the hostel. The game was a great antidote for George after his letter writing - it made him think about something else. It tested his arithmetic, which was a great source of pride for him. George and Danny would play quietly for the remainder of the evening.

At 11 o'clock the staff would start shooing them upstairs for bed but George and Danny would always seem to time their games to finish without winding the staff up and they would make their weary way upstairs to bed.

George hated this part of the day, as it was always when he was in bed, before he dropped off to sleep, that the memories of that terrible day would flood back. It would start with the faux bonhomie of the pub and would end with the yearning for the day that he could write his letter and move on as the pastor told him. His mind would churn over and over the death of his son and his imprisonment for manslaughter, the label of child killer in prison and the suicide of his wife. If he let it, the feelings would overwhelm him with thoughts of following the example of his wife. The only thing that stopped him was his one crumb of comfort, remembering his sole act of virtue on that terrible day.

63

George had a letter in his pocket explaining that to his son. When things got very bad and he felt completely lost he would get it out and read it. Tonight was shaping to be one of those nights and he knew exactly where to get the letter if he needed it.

George struggled to sleep and the tears formed, as he saw in his mind the mirror at the bottom of the stairs. The vision was always the same: his reflection sat there holding the lifeless body of his son as the police and the ambulance crew banged and shouted at the door. They had broken in and the memories all blurred - the confession to assuage his guilt as he admitted his drinking and told them that he was responsible. Later his little boy's body was put in the ground and he recalled watching in handcuffs as Tom's little coffin was placed in the grave.

Later came the plea of guilty to manslaughter and every single day of his seven year sentence seemed to merge into one.

Tonight George had to read his letter - he needed the tiny bit of comfort it offered. Pulling the tear-stained, creased and worn paper from his pocket, he read his own words.

Dear Tommy,

I have tried to write this so many times and I can't say sorry enough. I will never forgive myself for what happened. The Pastor says that if I believe you have gone to heaven then you will feel my pain and forgive me. I hope that is true and that one day I will see you soon and see that for myself. I know that if I had not been drinking you and Mummy would be alive today. I know that you would have grown to be a fine strong boy.

I know that you are with Mummy now and that she will look after you. I know that you will forgive her and let her find comfort. I love you little man and I hope that the angels are looking after you and Mummy. Tell her I understand why she felt that she could not carry on, and tell her that I love her and I am sorry that I was not there for her when she needed me. The only thing that keeps me going is the fact that at least my confession spared her from prison. Sadly, she could not find any peace and needed to be with you. I just hope that she can forgive me for being in the pub that night and I couldn't stop her from hurting you so badly that you died.

I love you my darling boy,

Daddy.

George cried as usual when he read it, wishing that one day it would, as Danny said, give his head peace.

Fuddamucker

THOMAS McGOVERN

A travelling salesman called Hank Lucas was driving fast along the roads of South Virginia, hurrying to keep an appointment with a local shoot shop owner. In a former life he'd had a successful business but that had tanked when the dotcom bubble had burst: his career had plummeted while his wife's soared - their marriage was just another casualty of the fallout. Hank's wife was a complete dream who turned into a nightmare before his eyes. Now he lived a fleapit existence, supporting his ex-wife and son by trying to sell guns to Hicksville gun and ammo stores. His sales were lousy and he had a meeting with his manager later today which would probably end with him getting fired.

He was speeding around the next corner when he saw a very short man with long hair and a bushy beard dressed in fancy dress like some kind of a wizard's costume and standing directly in his path. He stood on the brakes but knew he was going to hit him. The man on the road didn't look shocked at the oncoming vehicle, just generally bad tempered with the whole world. Short-arse stared directly at Hank and never tried to avoid the collision but waved his hand once at the oncoming car. Immediately behind the strange man a spiralling void opened in the sky and before he could scream at what was happening his car lifted from the road and tumbled before it was swallowed up.

In the land of Fairlyis the cloudy sun rose slowly over the kingdom – a land that had been bewitched for years: the crops constantly failed without reason and disease plagued the countryside. A constant haze enveloped the kingdom causing sickness and despair in people's hearts.

In this once fair land King Ogan ruled with an iron fist and put many to the sword - most at his personal whim or as sport for the baying crowd. The King's elite guards roamed the kingdom enforcing tithe collection from the population that left many with little to feed themselves. Any form of dissent was put down with brutal force; uprisings were savagely ended with everybody in the locality slaughtered and left as a message to neighbouring leaders and their communities. Ogan's knights also plundered the wealth of other kingdoms. Their hoard was gathered and taken to Ember Mountain where it was guarded by the fire-breathing Grinnock.

In one of the small villages of the kingdom Morbin, the chief tithe collector, was roaring the details of the next collection to the weary villagers and the consequences if they did not pay. Above him in the sky a swirling void appeared. He was bellowing orders to the populace when a battered car tumbled from the void and landed on his head. The crowd erupted into cheers but quickly stopped, fearful they would suffer for celebrating the death of the loathsome Morbin.

It wasn't long before the elite guards arrived. A dozen horse mounted armoured men dragged the comatose Hank from his metal chariot, tied him to a horse and galloped off towards the royal castle where he was dragged, bound in manacles and chains, before the king and his court. The throne room was full with those who had heard the news of this strange man's arrival and they looked forward to the afternoon's sport of quizzing the prisoner.

King Ogan looked coldly at Hank as various people from the kingdom were brought forward with questions for him. They asked if he was a spy from Otherland. Why did he kill Morbin? On and on it went. Later, masked men entered the throne room and looked the man over as they poked and prodded him, saying nothing. These were the King's inquisitors.

It was fairy Mando, the court couturier, who saved him from their bloody hands by asking, "Are you good at dragon slaying?"

The king approved with an agreeable grunt and before Hank could say *Alakazam* he was encased in a tailored suit of armour and handed a heavy sword before being escorted towards Ember Mountain on horseback. His mount was loaded with provisions including a requested box from his car. Mando rode alongside telling him a mix of court gossip and the dilemmas of his love life. Then he told him about the kingdom and its ruler.

"If I hadn't mentioned the dragon you would be dead by now at the hands of the inquisitors," he confided. The choice was go to the top of Ember Mountain after first avoiding the giant troll and passing the

Waterfall of Baine without looking directly into its waters: to do so drives anybody mad. All this before reaching the mountain top and defeating the fire-breathing Grinnock.

"What you must remember," continued Mando before leaving him at the approach to the mountain, "is that the troll has very good hearing but is stupid and easy to fool. The waterfall of Baine cannot be looked at directly: its like looking into your very soul. The waters reflect back every defect magnified to those caught by its gaze. It sends most of them completely mad. Whispers in the kingdom say the dragon's bark is much worse than its bite… and beware of everything else up there," he pointed to the mountain ahead of them. Then he turned his horse around, wished Hank the best of luck and left him.

Hank knew that with the number of sentries guarding the mountain he wouldn't have much chance of making an escape. His current situation was better than being boiled in oil but only marginally. He galloped towards the woods beside the base of the mountain where he dismounted and removed the suit of armour. He heard the creature before eyeballing him as the troll had developed the habit of talking to himself after years living alone. The troll was complaining to himself about the weather and why couldn't he find some proper food instead of living on berries and grass. Hank looked over the boulder he was hiding behind. The monster was more than twice his size and covered from head to toe in mangled brown hair.

"I will share my food with you, troll," said Hank.

The troll seemed more scared of the sound of Hank's voice than Hank was of the creature. The troll thought and then replied, "I could eat you and then eat your food."

Hank emerged from hiding chewing on the end of a drumstick as he stood in front of the troll. "Then you're going to have to catch me first, troll."

The chase lasted for an hour before the troll sat down exhausted. It had been easy to avoid him in the nearby boulder field. Hank realised that the troll looked malnourished as he offered him half a chicken. The troll accepted and Hank kept giving him more food until there was none left. After they had eaten they sat beside a roaring fire, smoking clay pipes outside the troll's dwelling – a hut made from branches and leaves. The creature told him that the king's guards gave him food on condition he stopped anyone going up the mountain. "I wouldn't really have eaten you," said the troll, "but they beat me."

Hank fell asleep listening to the troll's stories wondering if he would ever wake up again. When he did it was just before dawn and the troll was snoring. He stretched and yawned and began walking up Ember Mountain. In the dawn's early light he arrived at the ledge that passed the Waterfall of Baine and negotiated the path looking out of the edge of his vision where he could hear the water tumbling to his right. Even without looking directly at the waters he was still overwhelmed with feelings of self loathing and failure. There was something deeper forcing him to stare into the gushing waters as if he knew it would take away all the pain he had ever felt. Hank jammed his hand into his pocket and pulled out his Mp3 player and earphones. He hit *PLAY* as he stuck the ear phones in and closed his eyes. He kept moving slowly along the path only opening his eyes fully when the next Black Keys song started playing. As he pulled the phones from his ears he heard the noise of the waterfall behind him.

He crept slowly towards the fog-hugged submit, hiding and listening. He realised he wasn't alone up there. Around him moved some of the elite guards who were waiting for him, weapons drawn. He looked above himself to the mountain top where a large roar erupted and flames shot out sporadically. The smoke and mist provided good cover as he ascended further up the slope.

Hank thought he would have been more shocked at how easily he killed the first guard. The knight's sword clattered off the rock beside him: another hair's breadth and it would have been embedded in him. Hank pointed the barrel of the Colt commando rifle at the guard and squeezed the trigger. The gun jerked as it fired a short burst of gunfire into his body. A pink haze of blood briefly enveloped the knight who fell dead at Hank's feet. No wonder all those rednecks loved this gun. He sold a few every trip so he always had a demo model with him. He quickly took cover as two other guards ran over to their fallen friend, wielding swords and looking around them.

He slid the setting on the rifle to semi-automatic fire and scolded himself for wasting so many bullets on the guard who struck out at him. A single shot hit the nearest one smack in the face which disintegrated as he fell. The other charged at Hank but didn't manage five steps before being flung back with a chest wound. Hank walked over to the knight and shot him in the head. He didn't want any of them to suffer and this way they couldn't tell the other guards where he was.

He ran and hid behind a gorse bush to observe how many more guards were there and the best way to pick them off. Every time one revealed himself on the mountain above Hank shot him. Five…six…seven. This was easy. The last three guards didn't stay to add to their numbers - spooked by their colleagues suddenly dropping they ran from their location near the mountain top.

Hank crawled out from behind the bush to where he could see the summit. In the variable mist he heard nothing except the sound of his shoes on the mountain scree until a roar erupted nearby and flames bellowed into the sky. The sound was deafening but seemed unnatural. Suddenly the sound of his Colt echoed around the mountain top. The roars and flames of the dragon stopped as two men ran from beside the beast. Now it made sense to Hank as he approached the fire king. Before him was a very mechanical monster powered by steam with a flame thrower at its heart.

Hank walked around the back of the idling creature and pulled a large metal switch up; the creature's head fell to one side and its last hydraulic breath wheezed out before the mountain returned to silence. Hank sat down resting his back against the dragon's metal head. He had won this battle but it would mean war with King Ogan. For the first time Hank knew exactly what he was going to do: no more indecision. He felt relaxed as this realisation washed over him. He would make that king beg for mercy since he didn't heed any cries from his subjects. His guards would be the biggest obstacle in overthrowing this despot but Hank had decided to turn this place upside down.

Hank was reloading his rifle when the sky swirled above him and in the centre of the vortex was the little wizard he had nearly run down earlier that morning. The wizard was muttering to himself about those no-fun fuddamuckers when he swiftly punched Hank in the gut and grabbed him by the collar, preparing to shove him into the vortex when a sudden shot rang out on the mountain. The wizard was doubled in pain over his bleeding foot. Hank grabbed him and held him up so he was at his eye level.

"Now, my little humpy friend, you're gonna help me with a little regime change around here ...and then you're gonna get me home. I have a manager you should meet."

With this Hank jammed the gun in the wizard's face and flung both of them into the void which rapidly faded from the pale blue sky.

Getting To The Bottom of Things

TONY BRADY

There was a time in the 1970's when I was guaranteed a free lunch and Christmas Dinner. It was Luigi Vostronni's way of expressing his eternal thanks for solving a particular problem involving his business. He owned a trattoria in Hammersmith Broadway, North West London, and the problem I had solved for him was Boris, and although Boris had never actually dined in Luigi's he had his own methods for obtaining the price of a meal.

Boris was homeless: he lived rough in the area and survived by begging. He had a particular stratagem which he employed mainly in the summer months during the local office workers' lunch hour, or in the evenings. He would position himself near the entrance to Luigi's and put his hand out as prospective diners made their way to the entrance doors. Women were always the best target for his beseeching expression: their escorting partners invariably coughed up. Boris never spoke. Rumour had it that he was marooned in the area when a circus he worked in had moved on without him. When given money he bowed in gratitude, but for those who ignored him he had another response.

As they entered the restaurant, Boris would follow their progress through the front window of Luigi's that ran along the pavement to their table, which would invariably be by the window. Once they were seated, Boris would approach the glass and scowl at them as they scanned the menu. Then he would turn about and rest his back against the window. Very slowly he would then ease his trousers down, while making sure he did not reveal the front of his body, then he would bend forward and wriggle his exposed buttocks inches away from the diners' faces. The effect was either merriment or disgust and always resulted in Luigi's fury. However, as fast as he rushed out to remonstrate with Boris, the beggar's trousers were quickly restored and he would be re-positioned with his hand outstretched to accept the reward of the amused customers as they left the premises.

The local police told Luigi that Boris could only be "done" for *frontal exposure*. No-one had ever actually complained and Boris always behaved impeccably when the constabulary were about. He was known as "The Russian" down at the Station and was another neighbourhood eccentric. I helped to get him re-settled in a sheltered residential project in South East London – far from Luigi's restaurant, which was why its owner offered me the free meals.

I used to visit Boris but I never took him out to dine because there were no convenient cafés or restaurants in the area. I considered inviting him to Luigi's for Christmas Dinner but knew I couldn't: as a public servant, I had to decline on grounds of civic duty. Besides, he would have had to go in disguise. Boris as Father Christmas? Now there's a thought.

Religious Convictions

TONY BRADY

In the 1970s I worked for a London borough as a housing officer and part of that job was to visit prisons as a lay visitor for a Prisoners' Aid charity.

On my first assignment I visited Pentonville Prison and was escorted to the Chaplain's Office to be introduced to representatives of the various denominations. I must have missed the winks and nods in the humorous banter but listened carefully as I was instructed about the opening question I was to ask the first prisoner I had to visit.

"He's a bit of a joker," I was told. "He's in and out, mainly for drunkenness, but he has no real criminal form," said the Senior Warder on the way to the cells. "Make sure you ask him the first question as instructed by the Chaplain."

There was no need for a reminder as I had carefully memorized it. The cell door was unlocked and the Warder shouted at the inmate to stand to attention and told him that he had a visitor from the Chaplain's Section. I entered and, while the Warder stood outside the half-closed cell door, I greeted the prisoner and asked the all-important question: "Have you any religious convictions?"

Without hesitating the man replied, "Well, I wouldn't be in here if I hadn't pinched the collection plate from a church and made off on the vicar's bike."

Survivor

GORDON WILLIAMS

Did I ever tell you about the time I worked on a ship looking for the wreck of the *Titanic?* It was in 1982: I had two months between hospital jobs and my wife had just run off with our gardener. I was really upset - I hate mowing the lawn. I phoned a shipping company in Liverpool and asked if they had any short-term jobs working on cruise ships: I fancied sailing around the Mediterranean and getting paid for it but the man there said they had nothing like that and had I done any diving? I told him I'd been in a few dives in Liverpool but that wasn't what he meant.

The only job they had was as medical officer on a ship searching for the wreck of the *Titanic.* The previous officer had gone off sick and they needed somebody quickly: could I fly out tomorrow? I had nothing else to do so I said *yes.* That night I packed some clothes, six bottles of suntan lotion and those books I'd always wanted to read: *War and Peace, Ulysses* and the *Kama Sutra.* I flew out to Florida; the 747 landed reasonably near Miami airport and the ship's captain picked me up.

He introduced himself as Sheridan C. Slogg IV, shaking my hand with a grip that nearly dislocated three fingers. Some men are built like Greek gods but Slogg was built like a Greek restaurant. He wore a huge pair of baggy shorts and an 8XL Hawaiian shirt that a family of four could have camped in. He drove me in his pick-up to the harbour on the Florida Keys and welcomed me onto his ship which sat two inches lower in the water when he walked on board. I hoped he never went swimming in the sea – a passing ship might have tried to harpoon him.

That afternoon we sailed from the harbour, past a rowing boat that was going round in circles. We later discovered that a Lithuanian man had mistranslated the phrase *rowing across the Atlantic single-handed* from his Lithuanian-English phrasebook.

Captain Slogg proudly showed me around his ship - the *Nebulous.* It was very well equipped with a bathyscaphe, sonar, a gym, underwater surveillance cameras, two auxiliary inflatable craft, a decompression chamber and the best-stocked bar I'd ever seen. Then he introduced me to the crew – it was the early 80's and they all had beards, except the cook. She had a moustache. I asked what had happened to the previous medical officer and Slogg changed the subject to show me the decompression chamber. It was my job to assess everybody's fitness and to supervise the use of the chamber when they returned from diving.

There wasn't much else for me to do: a daily survey of minor illnesses and injuries took less than half an hour. The rest of the day was all mine. I started writing my autobiography but soon gave it up – I needed a better subject. I lay on my bunk contemplating the meaning of life and those deep philosophical questions that would sometimes trouble me: did Pavlov's dogs join the Salivation Army? Can acupuncture cure people of pins and needles? If a fat chance went on a diet, would it become a slim chance?

I was getting paid for this but I needed something else to fill my days and nights. One of the crew told me that the previous medical officer had experienced similar problems on the ship and after two months of relentless boredom and inactivity he had succumbed to the nautical version of cabin fever, locking himself in his cabin and refusing to come out. For five days he'd only eaten pancakes because that was the only food that the crew could slide under his cabin door. Things got more desperate and he'd been singing *Old Man River* non-stop for nearly two days, so they broke down his cabin door to find a wreck: not the wreck they had been searching for but a wittering shell of a man who had lost his grip on reality. Their quest for the *Titanic* was temporarily abandoned as they took him back to port and, because regulations required a medical officer on board, they needed an urgent replacement. That's why I'd got the job.

I lay on my bunk thinking: had I run away from my problems on land to face even worse problems at sea? Do vandals come from broken homes? Do fossils meet through carbon dating agencies? Tote that barge, lift that bale …Was I… was I – like my predecessor and Coleridge's *Ancient Mariner* – slowly going mad? I instigated a programme of physical and mental activity to stave off impending insanity: I jogged round the deck six times a day, lifted weights in the gym, played poker with the crew and started reading.

Fortunately, after another two weeks at sea the crew finally found the wreck of the *Titanic*. By then, I'd lost a stone, was down two hundred dollars and I'd nearly finished the *Kama Sutra*. After their initial celebrations in and out of the bar, the crew spent several days going down to the seabed in the manned bathyscaphe to install cameras around the wreck and we stood around a bank of monitors watching the images they transmitted. We were the first people to see the *Titanic* for nearly seventy years, watching pictures of the broken vessel encrusted with barnacles and sheathed with fronds of waving seaweed. Fish of all sizes swam amongst the wreckage which was still intact and recognisable in places. On the third day of looking at the monitors one of the crew shouted, "There's a man down there."

I thought he had been at sea too long, or in the bar too long, and asked, "Yeah, what's he doing?" and he said, "Playing the violin."

The crew crowded round his monitor and watched with open mouths: there, down in the hull was an elderly man with white hair, dressed in a dinner jacket. He *was* playing the violin. The captain immediately decided to rescue him and would have gone down in the bathyscaphe himself if he could have got through its door. Fortunately, the first mate offered to go down to the wreck and attempt the rescue. It was difficult, it was delicate and it was dangerous but he succeeded in transferring the white-haired man through the air-lock into the bathyscaphe and bringing him back slowly to the surface over three days to avoid him getting the bends. Then, after his five days in the decompression chamber, I examined him. He was in good shape for a man of his age.

He sat in the dining room, wearing a pair of sunglasses that the crew had given him to avoid the daylight he hadn't experienced for so long. He told us he was called David Jones and he was five years old when he had sailed with his parents on the *Titanic's* maiden voyage in 1912. His father was going to America to take up a post as second violin with the Boston Symphony Orchestra and he'd been separated from his mother in the rush for the lifeboats when the ship started sinking. He'd held on to his father's hand as the ship went down and they were trapped together in a large air pocket near the kitchen. They lived on the food there until it ran out; then they lived on raw fish and squid that they caught, along with water from the ship's tanks. His father had taught him to play the violin using instruments abandoned by the ship's orchestra and they wore the musicians' uniforms and dinner jackets. He had played duets with his father for many years but, sadly, had only been able to play solo after his father had died some time earlier.

We gave him his first cooked meal for decades; he was surprised at the taste of cooked fish but he finished it off. Then he picked up his beloved violin, which he'd insisted on bringing with him. He played us some Chopin: Preludes 18 and 43. Or was it 42? – I always get them mixed up. No matter – it was exquisite: note-perfect, heartfelt and passionate. The crew were moved to tears. They applauded Mr Jones and he asked if we could play him some music, so some of the crew went off to fetch their tapes. Unfortunately, when he heard Rap music for the first time he ran out screaming and jumped back overboard. We searched the area for three days but never saw him again. Captain Slogg swore us all to secrecy never to talk about Mr Jones; I met him at a reunion a few years later and the episode with Mr Jones had affected him badly: he was a shadow of his former self and down to only twenty eight stones. And it's been preying on my mind for a long time, too – I feel better after telling you about it today.

Did I ever tell you about the time I won the racehorse Shergar in a poker game with Elvis, Lord Lucan, a leprechaun and the Abominable Snowman on board the *Marie Celeste?* You've got to go? Well, maybe another time.

Poetry

Potato Apple Bread

ANGELA McCABE

I slice the apples thin
Mother guides my knife
Almost like a wafer

She mashes floury potatoes
Which have been sitting all day
On a ledge to cool in the breeze.

Dusts the board white
A snow of floured hands
Knead and pat

Second nature to her
As the rhythm of
The rolling pin.

She lays the Bramley slices
On the flat bread
Adds a dash of sugar

Another layer of potato dough
In a flash the cake is swung
From board to griddle.

Movements, timing exact.
Her deft hands turn the bread
Sacred as communion.

With calm and reverence
The cooling tray is stacked.
Offerings for the family.

Breakfast time, early morning
Father eats in sacred silence
Nourished by her love.

Lough Neagh Breeze

ANGELA McCABE

We walked past the rowan trees
With the Lough Neagh breeze
At our backs.

The promise of home
Still distant in the crimson sky,
The dimming light arrived too soon.

The scutch grass caressed
Our ankles as we ran barefoot
On dried out bogs.

A far off wail
"The Banshee" - the boys shouted.
We quickened our steps.

The yellow loaning
Was hard under our feet
The threat of death imminent.

No words spoken now
As each child turned into his lane
We ran the longest one.

Who would it be?
My mother my father or me?
Dusk enveloped our townland,

Onto the final sprint and home.
"We saw her, the Banshee."
Mother cut the bread

And shook her head
Buttered scones and fried pollans
"Eat your meal and shush" she said.

In bed we listened
For more lonely shrieks
As wind whistled through the rowans.

Hughie in the Hedge

ANGELA McCABE

Hughie lived in a hedge
Sometimes he stood in it
And sometimes he hunkered down
Often he scratched one leg with his foot
Then he'd scratch the other.

He wore a suit and a flat cap.
Once they were brown
Then they were green, like the hedge,
From moss and dew and wet.

When it rained
Hughie put his collar up
And turned his cap back
So that the rain ran down the peak.

Sometimes I'd forget about Hughie
In the hedge as I cycled by.

Then he'd step out – just one step
And say – That's a grand bike.

I'd stop and stand and we'd stare
At my Raleigh together.

With hands of green
He'd touch the handlebars.

Then he'd pat our dog Rover
And say – That's a grand dog.

Sometimes he'd take dry batch bread
And scallions and wisps of corn
From his pocket and chew on them
With rotting teeth.

Then one day as I went by
His spot was empty.
Hughie had died right there.

The next spring primroses and corn
Grew where Hughie had stood.

Sliabh an Iareann (The Mountain)

ANGELA McCABE

Morning mist, trees in a row
As if they had been painted
By Cezanne or Derain.

Patchwork of fields in different shades
Of mauve – the colour that some men say
Doesn't exist.

Cinnamon, saffron, nutmeg
Cake of granite, rendered and folded
Changing minute by minute in a reflective sun

Cloud above to tease you
Move, dance and turn again
And fog your grey blue hue.

Some people meditate by the sea,
But you are far from the ocean
No waves to erode you.

To contemplate in front of you
And send a silent prayer to Heaven
Reminds us of a stillness long forgotten.

Wrinkled summit like the faces
Of wise and silent men and women
Who give all through steady endurance.

Risen sun reflects off white rock
Like an oyster pearl glistening under the sea
Turns to a morning star new risen.

Translucent white cloud passes over
And carries on, leaving us to catch
Glimpses of you, hour by hour.

You are there in our mornings,
At our Angelus, our nights
And in our daily plights.

We go to your ridge.
No endless chatter here
Silence, save the bleat of sheep.

And if we could live as you
Cloud by cloud, sunset by sunset
We might know what it is to be still.

Fairy Piping

DIANE JARDEL

I was woken last night
From my slumber
By the plaintive cry of pipe music
The sound rose and fell
Weaving itself around the storm
The water crashed
Against the sea wall
Near the field where I lay

This sound must be part
Of the local legends
Of magic fairy piping
And children stolen away
Or swapped
My mother had always joked
That I was a changeling
As she gazed at my pointed ears

Could I be part of this ancient race?
As I stood at the window
And felt the breath of the mountains.
Could I go dancing up to the hills
And find my way into a fairy cave?

Did you hear the terrible storm last night?
The hail stones were enormous
Rattling the windows

No – I just heard the sound of fairy piping

That was just the wind, they said
Rattling through the rigging
Of the boats in the harbour

I smiled to myself
I was a changeling then

5 a.m. Blues

DIANE JARDEL

Sitting here
Clock ticking
Tap dripping
Fridge buzzing
Stomach rumbling
Nose freezing
Ears twitching
When does the peace come blazing in?

Sitting here
Head aching
Phone blinking
Birds tweeting
Heart thumping
Feet freezing
Eyes watering
When does the gladness zoom into my being?

Standing here
Body leaning
Brain ticking
Fingers grasping
Kettle boiling
Tea brewing
Porridge waiting
When does it all make sense?

The Mirror

DIANE JARDEL

I gazed into the mirror as a child
Pulling myself up to see
Blond hair and brown eyes
Mouth in a hesitant smile
The only one
I could tell how I felt
Or remembered how life had been
And promised how life could be

I looked into the mirror as a teenager
I saw a moon face
Full of blemishes, discordant
And sought to use it as a canvas
To paint myself more
Acceptable eyes and mouth
No truth was available
I imagined a fantasy of light and laughter
Of dance and friends
Of knowledge and wisdom

I glanced at myself in the mirror as a mother
I saw tired eyes
The satisfaction of creativity
No time to see myself separate
Two girls to hold my arms
One boy to treasure.
A home to make into a nest

Tired nights, happy days
Wondering at life's chances

As a mature woman
I see a stranger
A face that is different
Some angles there
A whole life in my eyes
Of failures and triumphs
Stress and peace
Weariness and euphoria
Sorrow and joy

Confident to let the world
See me as I am
Having found a life where I can feel real
The dreary depths of depression and fear
Have become occasional shallow troughs
Until I can remember the life
The child has now inherited
A life less rushed
Then enjoyed richly

Forty Years and Forty Nights

DERMOT MAGUIRE

Our father
(Who may be in heaven)
One Lent
Decided to read
The Holy Bible
Every night
For one hour
From eight until
The News at Nine.
But really I am not sure
If it was for one hour
Or for twenty pages –
He was doing it in stages.

He was doing it
For Lent
So it must have meant
A penance.
As it turned out
It was us,
Not him,
Who suffered most.
If we talked loud
He read louder,
And if we jumped about
He put us out.

'In the beginning

God created the heavens
And the earth.'
Were the first words
Father read
Out loud to us all.
Then Adam and Eve
And the apple,
And we wondered
If it was Grenadier,
Beauty of Bath
Or Cox's Pippin -
All the ones we had
In our orchard.

And how,
In the Name of God,
Could Methuselah
Have lived so long –
Nine hundred and sixty nine years!
We wondered
If it was a misprint,
Or, if he had spent
Most of it
Lying on his back,
Or, if it was some lack
Of faith
On our part.
Methuselah must have smelt
Something serious,
We joked,
Holding our noses
And Mother put her finger

To her lips.

Father told us
To be quiet
And have respect,
And louder he read
Until Noah
Built his ark,
As directed by God.
And the flood covered
The highest mountain,
Far greater than our flood
Of nineteen fifty three
When we had to go
To school in a boat.

The next night
We heard of
Abraham and Isaac
Jacob and Joseph
But our interest waned
Long before
The News at Nine.

Moses came the third night
In a basket, floating,
In the reeds.
We enjoyed the plagues
That God sent -
Especially the frogs,
And the gnats.
We had our own gnats

Up the road –
The gnats Cassidy's
We called them.

The locusts and the flies
And all the other pestilences
Came with fearsome devastation,
And we were dumb-struck
At the great dividing
Of the waters.

After three nights
The Jews had reached
The Promised Land.
But after that we gave up -
Just scraps here and there.

The Ten Commandments
On the mount:
Thou shalt not kill
Thou shalt not steal!
Robbing orchards
We reckoned
Didn't count.

There was the Law,
About this and that
But for us
It meant a light
On your bicycle.

Night after night

For forty nights
For heavens sake!

One night he read
How the walls of Jericho
Fell down.

Another night
How Jonah was three days
In the belly of the whale -
It was then, we sensed,
(Or were even relieved)
That the Bible wasn't really
Something to be believed.

And page after page,
Another night he read aloud
Of Daniel in the lion's den,
And we could see
The circus man
In the lion's cage.

Just when we thought
It would never end,
The big book
Was closed
And put away
In its special box
In the bottom drawer
In the press
Under the stairs.

And there it lay
For forty years, until
The Renovation,
When our house
Was born again.

Any Given Sunday In God's Own Country

JOHN JAMES

A golden shaft of pure light cleft the hills,
Dawn flooded the valleys and filled the dells.
A cock greeted it with its crowing cry.
'Feck you, yer feathered bollix!' the man sighed.
The man was known as Farmer Graham by name,
His dour mood and coarse language was his fame.
He heaved open the large old stable gate,
And tippy-toed over the cattle grate.
He then opened the shed to free the cows.
'Come by lassies – and less of yer old rows!'
One indolent young heifer would not rush,
He fetched a nonchalant kick up her tush.
She turned around and gave a mournful bray.
'Aye my love, I hear and know what you say.'
He made sure the field-gate latch was fast,
Before returning home for his breakfast
Mrs. Graham was gathering eggs from hens,
To serve with bacon, sausage for her men.
Two strapping boys and large grouchy husband,
Readying them for a day on the land.
Further down the lane in God's own country,
Past the wreck of the old devil struck tree,
There was a scattering of tiny cottages,
Parcelled off by tidy privet hedges.
One of them was pretty Tilly O'Shea's,
Who was ritually greeting the day.
Doing her callisthenics and whatnot,
It was Tai-Chi and all that other rot

She twisted her lithe frame this way and that,
Watched with boredom by her little black cat.
Watching too, was spotty Tommy Gorman,
From his window, peering through the gloamin',
Spiked ginger hair topped wide eyes at sill-level.
'Ger out of it! Yer heinous wee devil!'
'Ye'll go stone blind one of these fine days!'
Cried the Widow Gorman, wise to his ways.
Tommy then fled beneath his welcome quilt,
Shaking and shivering with fright and guilt.
She tsked and crossly pulled the curtains too,
Wondering how her misfortunes just grew.
The dawn sun rose an hour-notch in the sky,
Father Brennan eased up with a loud sigh,
Clasped his head, bemoaning the libation,
He had taken last night with Bishop Gren.
'Lord hath mercy on poor sinners like me!'
He muttered, then crossed himself guiltily.
He thought himself an ordinary man,
Not called by God, but pushed by his own clan.
Each generation a Brennan for the Cloth,
Yet 'Father Magoo' was the frequent scoff.
Myopia robbed him of due respect,
Despite possessing a fine intellect.
He kept it well hid and played the sad clown,
Chuckling at the rare bold kids in the town,
As they fled from the old Beetle he drove;
This was his last parish, no more to rove.
Ballygordonbaggot, named for a son
Of the land no doubt, but long forgotten,
Bally-go-on-and-bugger-it, so called
By the local wags, their plain humour so bold.

In this quiet town, that was oft by-passed
By the main road and then the tourist class.
Although not by the busy Kislovians;
Circassian blood ran through their proud veins,
Ran them here from the Tsar's dread killing band,
Through Turkey, Romania, Spain – now Ireland.
They rose *en famille* to re-stock the shelves,
Sunday newspapers and Saturday's loaves.
Aproned Pater, aloof grey eminence,
Giggling Mater gently broke the silence,
Sharing jokes with vivacious Viveka.
Already now the town's prime heartbreaker,
She was tall and graceful with a wasp's waist,
A flashing smile and eyes that made hearts race.
But it was all look and you dare not linger,
Unless you placed a ring on her finger.
In the town's stately white manse down the road,
Creeping downstairs was fragrant Mrs. Hoad,
Wincing at every creak of the old treads,
Not wishing to stir the monster in bed.
She glanced at her shiner in the hall glass,
Before shaky start to her Sunday tasks,
First to iron the bulky newspaper,
Praying fervently that there was no tear;
Then to squeeze the juice, put on eggs to boil,
With ten neat little soldiers, all loyal,
Then to escape the monster's dreadful wrath,
She would quickly run his steaming hot bath.
Before readying for Morning Church Service,
Treating her bruise with arnica poultice,
And covering it with make-up and veil,
To give no sign and to tell no sad tale.

For the monster was JP in the town,
Often clothed in his powdered wig and gown.
In a tiny tithe-cottage down further,
Breakfasting together were the Werthers.
Like two tiny wizened shrew-like critters,
Huddled in dressing-gowns and old slippers.
His Sunday Best suit and her floral dress,
Neatly draped on a sideboard, freshly pressed.
Father Brennan, after recovery brew,
His face now showing a much brighter hue,
Was clad in his many undergarments,
Awaiting his white surplice and vestments.
Like an actor preparing for the stage,
He then read his well-thumbed script, page by page.
He strove for a clear happy medium,
Between curt brevity and dread tedium.
Tilly O'Shea was now filling her crates,
Candles, pot pourri and hand-painted plates;
All natural, made by her own fair hand,
To sell at the market, at her small stand.
Joe Duffy polishes his old oak bar,
In the town's friendly pub – *The Morning Star*.
Ready for kick-off at past Sunday noon,
Only the Bar, mind you, not the saloon.
He and the Father had an arrangement
- All made with JP Hoad's crucial assent –
By noon's strike, Father Brennan's service ceased,
By 12.05, Joe Duffy was released
To throw open the rose-red public doors,
In due accordance with ancient bye-laws.
Tommy Gorman had escaped his Ma's leash,
To play soccer and disturb the peace.

He thought himself too old for Sunday School,
Besides, it was boring and so uncool.
His Ma gave up on her vain, fruitless search,
And began to prepare herself for Church.
In his chill vestry stood Father Brennan,
He peered in the glass at a blurry man,
Then checked his glasses were in the pulpit;
Once, they'd been hid by that horrid wee shit,
Tommy Gorman, when he was altar boy,
One April first, causing both mirth and joy.
He had to blag his way through the sermon,
Cursing Tommy's soul to Armageddon.
The bells rang out their clarion call,
Commanding the righteous, stirring their gall;
And sinners to begin their penitence,
But from most now there'd be indifference.
He went to greet his pious parishioners,
Arriving there first the doughty old Werthers,
Immaculately turned out as usual;
More Sunday regulars heeded the bell,
Followed by tawdry drizzle of others,
Before the sedate Hoads, her clad in furs.
Tardily came breathless Mrs. Gorman,
Apologies shushed by Father Brennan.
Tilly O'Shea had no time for Church,
Which put men first on a lofty high perch.
She was New Age and all things feminine,
Green-shaded and humanitarian.
Her temple was her own pure sylph-like form,
Attracting male worshippers the sad norm.
However, not one would she entertain,
Till her expectations they could attain.

It was said she had been a wild thing
In Dublin town, when she'd first taken wing.
But now she was more settled with herself,
Clean living, little money, but good health.
She mounts her antiquated bicycle,
And with loaded trailer rode down the hill,
Towards the quiet, peaceful Town Hall Square;
Where local people would soon gather there,
For Sunday afternoon Open Market,
The car forgotten – no room to park it.
Tilly arrived early to set her stall,
Others had the same notion, traders all.
She quietly placed her wares, no panic.
Then she reserved meat and greens, all organic,
From her fellow traders, all amicable,
All seemed eager for the nascent rabble.
Joe Duffy carefully undid the locks,
Then placed outside the grubby red sand-box,
For the smokers and their cigarette ends,
The smoking ban, a rule he could not bend.
Even though the regulars fulminate,
Eternal nicotine habits to sate.
Fair weather or foul, they'd all traipse outside,
With their heads bowed and pocketing their pride.
His first customer was old Con Maguire,
Shuffling to his usual seat by the fire.
Joe had readied a tumbler of whiskey
And a little jug of water, ice-free.
No spoken thanks could Joe ever discern,
Old Con Maguire was usually taciturn.
Other regulars joined Joe at the bar,
Noise was now rising in *The Morning Star*.

105

Dapper Mr. Werther came in then,
To have a pint with the other old men.
But for him, it would only be the one,
All kind offers he would politely shun.
Paid for his own with a five euro note,
The change for the poor-box or the lifeboat.
But Joe Duffy and good Father Brennan,
Conspired over this and the Church collection;
Each Christmas, a large hamper and turkey
For the Werthers, who had no family.
No money also but a fearsome pride,
Their parlous state they'd resolutely hide.
Charity they would warily accept,
As long their secret Father Brennan kept.
Chastened Tommy Gorman sat at the table,
His face downcast and looking miserable;
His Ma had given him a telling off,
Grounded him, afternoon soccer was off.
Sunday dinner to be eaten in silence,
Dessert only on his Ma's sufferance.
Down at the Hoad's it was all quiet too,
In the dining-room painted duck-egg blue;
Apart from Mr. Hoad's monotonous slurp
And then the occasional rumbling burp.
Mrs. Hoad found his manners quite uncouth,
And yet he was the charmer in his youth.
She did not know then the angry monster,
That lay within that so handsome outer.
Tilly nibbled on a celery stick,
Taking a break from the human traffic.
Rising when people seemed interested,
Smiling to get buyer and cash parted.

Her homemade wares made cheap and cheerful gifts,
The warm smells and bright colours gave a lift.
Mrs. Werther has Sunday meal ready,
Her husband arrived home a bit unsteady.
Alcohol and age conspired against him,
Robbing him of balance and youthful vim.
She soon settles him down promptly to eat,
They had purties, fresh greens, gravy and meat.
It may seem to some to be paltry fare,
But with age, appetite just isn't there.
McGreevey the butcher fills a full bag
Of good quality produce, not old scrag;
Just charging what he knows they can afford,
Slipping in odd goodies under the board.
Viveka in a shawl and summer dress,
Strolling in manner carefree and careless,
Ignoring all the countless turning heads,
Proposals of marriage remain unsaid.
Her basket slowly fills with market fare,
Her parents' prices just could not compare
The market traders paid peppercorn rents,
Unlike the burden borne by her parents.
Their own shop could not be run at a loss,
So no hard feelings, they would not be cross
The market was only there once a week,
And convenience most now would seek.
She paused and chatted to Tilly O'Shea,
They exchanged the gossip of the day.
Also gossiping, Mrs. Hoad and her friends,
In a summerhouse at the garden's end.
She sat in the shade, under a large hat,
On her lap there purred a dozy fat cat.

As she chatted away her current woes,
Careful not to give weapons to her foes.
She essayed a manner enigmatic,
Skipped any talk of the melodramatic.
JP Hoad was kept busy networking,
Real men had no time for idle chatting,
This was a lie he told all and himself,
Believed it truly a key to his wealth,
Attending Church was only decorum,
The Boardroom was his principal forum,
That and the Courthouse in which he oft reigned,
Delivering justice as if ordained.
Mr. Werther clad in slippers and pipe,
Fulfilling the mundane stereotype,
Had fallen asleep in his mothy chair.
His wife took his glasses and smoothed his hair,
Emptied his pipe and draped a cardigan,
Over his supine form, finally then
She sat down now to start her own knitting.
A long red woolly scarf she was making,
For Father Brennan and cold chilly days,
His frequent kindness she'd try to repay.
Tommy Gorman, all alone in his room,
Is playing his video-game "Kaboom!"
Wishing his Ma would give his head some peace,
It was nag, nag, nag, she just would not cease.
If only his father was still with them,
Then there would be no hassle, no problem.
His Ma was up there at the local shrine,
Ensuring "Our Lady" was looking fine.
They were seeking Vatican approval,
For recognition of the 'miracle';

The Madonna was seen to oscillate,
By a local nun and visiting Prelate.
Cynics cited the Communion wine,
Rather than sacred sign from the Divine.
Joe Duffy was shooing out customers,
Long after the bell for last orders.
He could now smell his Sunday roast,
The best for miles around, he'd often boast,
On behalf of his upstairs loving wife,
The best and brightest star in his sweet life.
Tilly O'Shea was packing up her stall,
A nearly empty trailer she would trawl,
Back up the hill to her tiny cottage,
With fresh meat and cheese for her ice-cold fridge,
Greens, pickle and jam for her small larder,
Thinking that her life could be much harder.
JP Hoad had ended his day's business,
Feet up, perusing the National Press,
Oft harrumphing at certain articles,
Concerning soft treatment for criminals.
Mrs. Hoad had said farewell to her guests,
Going back to the man that she detests.
She'd devise a new cunning strategy,
To ensure her evening was monster-free.
Widow Gorman had returned to housework,
Pointedly ignoring her bold young turk,
Who occupied himself with the same game,
His manner, for now, docile and tame.
Father Brennan returned from his visits
To the sick, offering them his comforts.
Today, he had narrowly missed a dog,
Almost pushed in a ditch by a road-hog;

Driving round was not getting easier,
Each day he would just avoid disaster.
Sister Gabriel was cooking dinner,
Angel Gabriel was what he called her.
The Kislovians pulled down the shutters,
Viveka would give no more heart flutters.
Their food would be perfumed and highly spiced,
No purties, but plenty of coloured rice.
Pater would start the meal with a short prayer,
Giving earnest thanks for the good food there.
Mrs. Werther packed up her keen knitting.
All the while her husband gently sleeping.
An early night tonight, after supper,
A few biscuits, a scone and a cuppa.
Tired Farmer Graham drove in his livestock,
And teased the arrogant old strutting cock.
His eldest boy held open the field gate,
His youngest kept the ambling cows straight;
Of both boys he was so very proud,
But these warm thoughts he never spoke aloud.
Mrs. Graham, whom he loved uppermost,
Was busy preparing the Sunday roast.
As the sun now sets on God's own country,
Ballygordonbaggot forever be.

But I'm Here

DIANNE TRIMBLE

In city pubs friends meet.
They laugh, talk and sing,
Not noticing time pass.
But I'm here.

On scorching beaches tourists lounge.
They doze, swim and tan,
Not noticing time pass.
But I'm here.

In concert halls music lovers sit.
They listen, hum and clap,
Not noticing time pass.
But I'm here.

Here, far from crowds, bustle and noise,
In the still countryside,
Noticing only the dimming light
That marks the evening's passing.

A Rosy or Real Past?

DIANNE TRIMBLE

I remember lounging in a Muskoka chair beside a lake on a hot summer day. Did mosquitoes feast on my bare arms as dusk fell?

I remember flitting across a pristine fluffy blanket of snow on a winter night. How often did I slither and fall, jarring my spine on this fresh coverlet?

I remember walking on a country road to the clip clop beat of Mennonite horses trotting by. Did blaring radios from passing cars disturb our time warp?

I remember watching the second language on Toronto's street signs change from Chinese to Korean to Polish as I travelled a streetcar's route. Did I feel a stranger in my own city?

I remember strolling across the moonlit campus, lost in my thoughts, oblivious to my surroundings. How often did I stop mid-stride as a skunk shuffled across my path?

I remember rushing along a muggy Toronto street, a busker's raucous song lightening my step. Did the suffocating heat ensnare me and break my stride?

I remember leaning on the polished rail of the Centre Island ferry, watching Toronto's skyscrapers recede as flat, serene parkland approached.

Did I long for the buzz of the frenetic grey jungle behind?

I remember a past comprised of golden moments.
Do I remember or imagine this distant world?

Betrothal

KATHARINE MAY

Would you
Add fuel to the fire
Pour petrol on the flames
Burn me,
Brand me on my forehead,
Tie me to the stool
Drown me
For knowing secrets
And keeping them

Would you steal
My pelt
Trap me
Ensnare me
Take me from the sea
And not allow me to
Return
The silkie
Heartbroken
Sealskin woman

Would you
Condemn my girl child to death
Or make her second best
Or would you value her
Equally
And love her and myself
Unconditionally?

Change of skin

KATHARINE MAY

I wanted to make you a suit
That couldn't be bought or sold.
The lining was love
And the cloth was my dreams,
Its buttons were stars
Moonlight shone in the seams.

I sewed all night in secret
So no-one would know
It was you that I loved.
I sewed all day
Until my fingers bled,
And blue
Became red.

I made you a suit
That couldn't be bought
Or sold.
But now your ghost stands before me
And I know the king of my heart
Is dead.

Summer of '83

KATHARINE MAY

Sitting in the bar no money not drinking,
Rough rattle of ferry boat
Carrying passengers like cattle crawling,
Deep disturbing noise, throbbing children crying,
On deck stargazing a sailing boat graceful,
Red and white mass of funnel belches grey smoke
Into the night.
Going North flat lowlands canals crisscross
The window of train moving,
Haarlem on a summer evening, brick streets and high houses.
Klein Heiligland. Little Holyland. Number 32.
Heirloom mattress for sleep.

Amsterdam: squares shadows cast by sunlight,
Narrow darkened streets
Wind along water. Java, Sumatra, Bali straat, little Indonesia.
The battle of Waterlooplein murals commemorate squatters' riots.
Dam square Japanese tourists rock band crowds fire eaters
Black musicians traditional jazz in the side streets pied piper like
Lead the hypnotised behind.

Dark against dark gothic old church *Paradiso*,
Nightbright faces shining lips contort messages,
Yellow and red walls envelop sweet drug smells
Plastic cups beer and whiskey eyes darting crossways
Tall windows diamond paned open to the hot darkness
Whiplash whitebright forked lightning

Rooftops flash into the night.

Bass boom slow and heavy pulse beat
Body drift in sound sway
Move back and forward focus on the stage, follow the play
Of darting dance shadows.
Harsh white light glare tired faces drawn
Sweat wet lost look to the floor. No more.

Soft rain falls on the street,
Cigarette haze at a bus stop,
The bus homeward nothing said.
"Chat-fou" last life-breath of the night
half-smiles as a glass falls slow motion smash
On the floor. Two girls dancing between tables:
Enter one man with a hat,
Smiles a leer and joins the dancers,
Shakes his sleeve and a white rat appears
Runs up his arm across his neck
One girl stops the dance in fear
The man leaves, his act complete.
Last drinks glasses tipped back
Chairs scrape across tiles
The drift out into the morning.

A grey day wild grasses
Bicycles through the dunes
Flowers yellow and purple orchids
Life begins inside the body breasts swell.

Tram across city to clinic,
Respectable traditional Dutch house,

White uniforms scrupulously clean nurses
Count notes fill in a form and wait.
Coffee available but no-one takes any.
Everyone looks at each other pretending not to.
Different faces. One girl on her own terrified look
So young like a 12 year old.
Appointment with Dr. Wong,
Small oriental perfect English,
Sumptuous shiny white chairs,
Coil, intra-uterine device,
Septicaemia of the womb. No thanks.
Belowstairs, a pair of disposable pants and cloth,
Sanitary towels for afterwards.
Small room cubicles, narrow bed with plastic cover
Partition walls a woman groans.
Waiting anticipation of pain bitter thoughts
Another room all white steel machines,
Legs apart on a couch nurse strokes arm talks softly
The local anaesthetic finished
A foetus five weeks old.
Back into the cubicle waves of tears,
Feel alone in pain.
Look for the metro station
Concrete underground platform greyness.

Shadow dancing candle flickering
Against the window pane. A fine line separates
Reflection and original
Indistinguishable now.
Slow side-stepping night haze full pregnant darkness
Anticipates the image:
Scheherezade, a sleep

Dream spelt mystery conjurors nightingales and
Emperors.

Blue mountain against grey sky
Hay sways in the cool wind blowing.

Sunflower

GRAINNE FARRELL

The wind tossed her mind like a puppeteer to feelings
Thunder and lightning piercing through her shattered heart
She sobbed beneath the shadows of impending clouds
Whilst rain beat against her anguished face
Snow and ice froze her to stormy beliefs
Fixing her to a tempestuous gloom
An infinite sky of unwavering sadness.

The sun rose again awakening her youthful senses
Thawing the impossible diamond ice
Small hopeful thoughts rang through her ears like bird song
Whilst Sunflowers blossomed where she lay
The colours of nature danced into her weary eyes
A rainbow of desires and dreams
Woe floated behind her like leaves in the autumn

Because without shadows, there cannot be light.

Untitled

GRAINNE FARRELL

Some believe I am sensitive,
Others insist I am ill,
I believe I am muted,
Hurry along with another pill.

She

GRAINNE FARRELL

Strong, yet supple
Silent and stubborn,
Her grace is powerful and her power is graceful
She stands alone among others and watches silently, as the earth revolves around her. Her body, a tower of nature, exquisite shape and fine detail, separates her from those surrounding,
She is unique.

Her wisdom and beauty are equal in bountiful measure,
I believe she is perfect,
Yet she is solemn witness to the imperfections of life.
She watches as others destroy this precious gift around her,
Sighs as life kills life.
Her delicate soul is shaken with sorrow while she tosses her head in the wind,
She groans when this ugly, hedonistic personality of life is unmasked.

While hollow pain haunts her inside,
Her outward beauty is cast onto undeserving others,
She never judges, but will never forgive
Despite the water running from her weary eyes, she stands elegant and proud,
Today she will focus on the positive
She will dance in the rain until she can welcome the sun once more.
She will stretch her long, graceful arms in the wind, waving goodbye to the storms.

No longer will she bow under the burden of life
She is glowing under the sunlight
Turning her every feature to absorb its shimmering rays, and smile into the sky.

She is dying
She has lived a long, arduous yet fulfilling life
Born amongst the joyful renaissance of spring
Basking in the sweltering glory of summer
Waving farewell to friends and family in autumn
And standing frozen and heroic throughout winter.
She will never forget the smiles she has given and been given.

She bows down for her final time in this late autumn dusk
Taking her last look at the products of her journey
The starlight reflects off her weakening body as she leans on whimpering family for support,
She falls with poise through eerie silence
Her fragile body broken and deformed on the ground beneath her
She will live hereafter through friends and family, growing with and within them.
She was and always will be a magnificent creature of nature:
The magnificent tree.

Baking Bread in the Bardo.

ANGELA McCABE

Bardo – liminal state
Life suspended
Bardo of life, of death, of dreams.

And so my mother passes
Into the Bardo of death
External constraints removed.

Light from the moon
Holds a mirror to the mind
Immediate luminosity.

Memories are a dream
I pray – be happy and lose attachment
To the things of life

Seven weeks, seven days
Seven prayers, seven mantras for
Pristine awareness.

I dream she is baking bread
In the bardo of becoming
Soda bread on the pan

Light, white, perfect soda farls.
My brother and I wait
salivating from the sweet smell.

She is wearing pink lipstick
And goes for a walk till the bread cools
Death suits her.

Happier and healthier
Than her last years in life
The release is liberating.

"To the end of birth is death
The end of meeting is parting
Death is the fate of all that lives"

I pray in my dreams
And wake to pray again
And wonder –

How did she do that?
My mouth waters in the kitchen
I bake bread in my bardo

Offer some to those gone before,
Before I eat
A white light soda farl.

But not as perfect
As those in her bardo
Not as sweetly scented.

Coat

ANGELA McCABE

"Will you make me a coat
That looks respectable and rich
Yet able to keep out
The winter of Eastern Tibet."

We began to make a coat
Gold brocade on the outside
Three linings on the inside.

Rabbit fur. Moss green wool,
And a silken peacock blue
For the final trim.

We stitched and tacked and tailored
And stayed up nights
Till we were sure

It would keep out the chill
of the winds, the cold of the snows
And still look respectable.

Finally we fitted him
With the coat before he left.
To top it, a matching hat.

Many months later
When the snows had melted
He returned without the coat.

He never intended to wear it
It was for the old man
High upon the plateau.

Outfit those in need like kings and queens
As you would serve a Deity
In silence, Rinpoche taught.

Autumn

ANGELA McCABE

Stormy turbulent days as autumn returns
Leaves fly through the villainous winds

The year grows old with a promise of
Snow in transient white grey clouds

From now on everything withers and dies.

Vigour in work and fruits of labour
Bring reward in the routine days

Rituals of the season
Time and space and honour

As the farmer gathers his crop.

Farther away on a different plane
Glory and shame can change in an instant

As the light turns to darkness
Or a warm breeze to a squall

Take comfort from the change of seasons.

The sun once set will return
And spread its brilliance

The moon once risen

Will shine a clear light

Nothing lasts forever
Not even the thorns and thistles of our time.

The Spirit Of Christmas

SEAMUS CAROLAN

The Boxing Night party was in full swing at Rooney's house. Oin Connolly, the legendary local fiddler, was playing a waltz, while keeping a careful eye on the bottle of stout at his left foot. The elderly neighbour, Hugh Pat, who had only come to hear Oin play, sat next to him on a milking stool, smoking a crooked pipe, with his back to the vertical stone at the side of the hearth fire. Now and again he shook the wetness out of the pipe shank onto the fire and followed this up with a good spit, which sizzled on the hot turf.

The women sat in a bunch between the dresser and the room door in the middle of the wall opposite the fire, and chatted among themselves. It was nervous, superficial chat: they were really taking stock of whatever eligible men were about and making sure that their own presence was noted.

There was a wide age spread in the group, from girls in their teens to mature ladies, still hoping to attract the attention of a suitable male. The old 'pishtrog' applied – a woman for every man and a man for every woman – with hope springing eternal.

The men were gathered round the jamb wall, filling the hall and even encroaching into the sitting room with the box beds along the wall. Most were talking about cattle and the weather, a fag in one hand and a bottle of stout in the other. They were also keeping a tight eye on what was evolving, and by whom. This was an opportunity to evaluate potential breeding arrangements and, with so few such opportunities, it was important to pay attention and make mental notes.

Jimmy The Dancer was in full flight, swirling round the flagstone floor with consummate ease. He could twist and turn, check and change direction better than a hunted hare, occasionally stamping his heel at the end of one of Oin's special wee decorative variations, added in to flesh out the basic tune. Their eyes would meet every now and again, in the mutual appreciation of the fiddler and the dancer, each reluctant to break the spell of the moment. Some of these tunes went back generations and Oin would

131

often reflect on the memories of his father and uncles who passed them on to him so many years ago.

Jimmy's dancing ability did not endear him to the women nor the men: his level of expertise and agility were regarded with suspicion. Where could he have learned to dance like this? No one carrying out a full programme of useful activity could have the time or energy to get that good. It had connotations of the travelling playboys and even the showman, Clary Hayden, couldn't dance like Jimmy.

However, Jimmy served a very useful purpose: at some stage during the night he would dance with every available woman thereby ensuring that each was paraded around the floor to be viewed from every angle by the, almost entirely, dance-shy men who could weigh up not the dancing ability but the general potential for childbearing, bucket carrying, egg gathering and cleaning, turf-catching and other necessary qualities which would be vital in a future wife. "I wouldn't want her for dancing," was the retort when one lady was declared not to be a great mover on the dance floor.

Jimmy was immaculately turned out in his white starched shirt and collar with a reddish patterned tie, complete with gold tie pin and cuff links. His navy trousers were pressed to a sharp edge and his black shoes gleamed as they reflected the light from the Tilley lamp on the wall and the glowing fire. He kept his hair nicely combed at intervals and regularly touched in the "Bing Crosby dinge" at the top right hand side. There was a faint whiff of Old Spice aftershave mixed with a tinge of Brylcreem.

The kitchen floor was spick and span for the occasion and even the old pot bag, which was placed under the lid on top of the boiling spuds to act as a condenser for the steam, had been removed from its usual resting place under the table to a temporary position behind the half door. By now it was wet, cold and dirty and possibly harbouring some slaters or worms which would seek refuge under the door, not to mention an assortment of spittles.

The lads around the door were getting into fine form at this stage - the stout having been augmented with regular swigs of poteen brought along to liven things up. One of them pointed to the pot bag and suggested that this would make a lovely scarf for Jimmy. The bag was lifted gingerly by the corners, held ready for the shoulders of the now reversing Jimmy and nicely draped around the spotless starched white shirt.

With the speed of a recoiling snake, Jimmy detached himself from his dancing partner and sent the offending object flying across the room in the direction of the seated ladies while immediately launching himself at the suspected perpetrator of the trouble among the crowd of lads, by now back-tracking fast towards the closed half-door. The flailing Jimmy was conveyed through the melee by a variety of thumps, elbows and pushes, then out over the half-door, ending up with his face in the water channel which carried all manner of waste water from the doorstep to the sheugh at the foot of the street. One of Jimmy's companions ploughed in and was quickly dispatched in a similar direction. Both men were in such a rage to get at the offenders that they pulled the half-door off its hinges, causing the whole bunch of men to spill out onto the street where an almighty row spread into the haggard via the turf-house, with one man ending up on his back on the dung hill.

Oin Connolly, as was his wont at the slightest indication of trouble, had gathered his bow, case, bottle of stout and fiddle, hooked it to the room and stayed there until the row was settled and order restored. When he was persuaded to come out and continue the music, the old man at the fire enquired, "Well Oin, what do you think of that for a carry on?"

Oin took a slug out of the bottle, twanged on the fiddle's strings with his thumb, his ear close to the stock, and replied, "It's like this, Hugh Pat - there would be no point in them being ignorant if they didn't show it."

The Dead House

KEN RAMSEY

The Dead House was in our territory. We were The Mill Street Gang and our territory ran from Mill Street up to the Ritz cinema, along by the Railway Yard, out the Irvinestown Road, round the Mill Lough, up over Rutherford's Hill, down to the hospital then round past the dump and back up over the Forthill and along the Convent hedge. Our territory had several other gang boundaries that were dangerous to stray too far over; The Back Street Gang, The Gasworks Gang and the Westville Gang guarded them against us. The countryside boundaries we left alone; beyond them were people who wore old clothes, spoke with funny voices and smelt of cattle. We knew our territory well and patrolled it regularly. We had many favourite haunts, which we would not share with any other gang. To achieve this goal we needed discipline and a gang leader.

Leo was the leader of the Mill Street Gang, even though no one knew why. We never had votes or an election for a gang leader, Leo said he started the gang so he was the boss, but that wasn't true - my big brother used to be in the gang long before Leo. He stayed the gang boss by bullying and using his henchmen Dermot and Dessie to beat up anyone who didn't behave the way he ordered them to. He had a range of punishments he used himself but always he had the henchmen with him. He loved pulling your hair or burning you with cigarettes or hot sticks from a fire; he'd throw you in the lough or a shough or worst of all he'd nip you really hard. If you fought back or squealed to your parents on him you would get the 'full treatment' from Dermot and Dessie. Despite all the bullying you still had to be in the gang - you couldn't play in gang territory if you weren't.

The Dead House was a regular haunt of ours. It sat between the hospital and the riverside on its own. It was a bleak, foreboding building. The door was kept closed but never locked. Inside it had a big room with a dull electric light bulb in an enamelled shade hanging from the high ceiling. The light was never turned off. It had a window with thin curtains always pulled together to keep the daylight low. All the walls were painted a dirty white or maybe it was light green. We were not interested in the décor; just the dead bodies covered in white sheets lying neatly along the walls. Its proper name was The Morgue but to The Mill Street Gang it was "The Dead House."

When you were younger and wanted to join the gang you had to do the Dead House Initiation Test. The gang would gather in the bushes a short distance away and out of sight from the hospital. First the gang made sure there were no living people visiting the dead people and when we had the 'all clear' we gathered outside the door. The aspiring member was told that to join the gang all he had to do was open the door, go into the Dead House alone, close the door behind him, cross the room between the dead bodies, touch the back wall opposite and come back out through the door. Some were so scared they couldn't run and slowly shuffled with every muscle tightly clenched and eyes ablaze across the room to the wall and then back outside. Others opened the door, galloped across the room, bounced off the wall and charged back out. There were no rules about how you did it but you couldn't be in the gang unless you did The Dead House Initiation Test.

After a few visits to the Dead House we got so used to the dead bodies that we would crowd in and lift the covers off their faces to see if we knew them. Many times we brought the news back to Mill Street about someone we all knew who was in the Dead House.

Sitting in the bushes one winter afternoon it was wee Damien who first asked Leo how he had done his Initiation Test - did he walk or did he run? Foolishly he stumbled over his answer and that gave the rest of us time to think. No one could remember Leo ever doing The Initiation Test. Suddenly we were all united by the one thought - he hadn't done the test! Our courage grew and rebellion beckoned. "Show us again,' we urged. Even Dermot and Dessie kept quiet.

The standoff lasted for nearly an hour. Leo said he had done it years ago before any of us were in the gang. Then he said he was the leader of the gang and didn't have to do it. His indignant protests were no good - wee Damien pressed home our advantage and challenged him to do it again - there and then. By now we were all sure Leo was afraid to be in the Dead House on his own. Hiding in the bushes close to the Dead House, the gang's rebellion against the leader rumbled to an ultimatum. Wee Damien's was the killer punch: surely if Leo was the gang leader we all should have seen him do it and if he wanted to stay the leader, and in the gang, he should show us how he'd done it the first time. Leo knew he was backed into a corner and had no choice but to show us all that he was the bravest and deserved to be the gang leader.

By now the winter light was fading, dusk was settling down fast and a mist from the river was creeping up towards us. Leo set off for the Dead House with all of the gang members on his heels. He ran up to the door, grabbed the handle, pulled it open and began his race to the far wall. He didn't close the door behind him and that wasn't fair so Willie jumped to close it, but just before he did Wee Damien ducked under his arm and switched the light out – plunging the Dead House into darkness.

You could hear Leo scream all over The Mill Street Gang's territory. You could hear him scream at the top of Coles Monument; you could hear him scream in Ballinamallard. We all heard him scream but we were far too busy trying to run flat out back to Mill Street and laugh like hyenas at the same time. They certainly heard him scream in the hospital: two doctors in white coats ran down to the Dead House thinking they had made a mistake and a corpse had come back to life. Leo never found the light switch and when the white-coated doctors opened the Dead House door just as he ran past it in the dark he passed out.

Leo spent that night in the hospital. It took hours to clean him up and calm him down. Even when he was allowed home he didn't leave his house for two days.

Leo was still the leader of The Mill Street Gang but now his leadership had changed. There were no more beatings or bullying - from then on he knew we could get him any time we wanted.

A Fairy Ring

CAIT VALLELY

"Will I give you another sausage, Pa Joe?"

"I'll have one, Mam, if you don't mind," said Dermot to his mother, who was standing behind P.J.'s shoulder, holding the frying pan in her hand, ready to land the sausage on his already heaped plate.

"Could you at least wait 'til I'm finished with your brother? Just because you are home on holidays doesn't mean I have to wait on you hand and foot."

As the mother gave out to Dermot she started to butter hot toast for P.J.

"Sorry, Mam, I'll get the breakfast myself. Sure, don't you have to go to yoga? Ya know, last night, some of the fellows in the pub were saying Sean Quinn went bust because he changed the dolmen from its place. Sure, I remember when he built the hotel; the ould ones kept saying he'd never have a day's luck. He shouldn't have moved the stone from where it always was."

His younger brother, P.J., looked up with a sneer.

"Pisreóg, Dermot, that's all that is. Just a superstition. You'd think you'd have got a bit of cop-on living in New York. It was gambling with Anglo Bank got Quinn into trouble, not the fairies."

"Fairies! P.J. - sure, you'd be an expert on them alright, especially the ones on Knockmullin. An expert at not going near them."

"That's enough out of you now, Dermot. P.J. was right not to go near that fairy ring. It's an easy place to fall and hurt yourself. Sure a neighbour of ours, Kevin Myers, was never right in the head after they found him unconscious up there. They say he was taking a shortcut home from the pub. He must have tripped and lain there all night. I am telling you, anything that came out of his mouth after that was pure nonsense. P.J. - didn't you want a lift into town? If you wait until I come back from my yoga class, I'll bring you in."

"Ah, Mam, that's too late. I have a sure winner in the 12 o'clock race. I want to place a few bob on it."

"Dermot, make yourself useful and bring your brother into town."

"But Mam, I was going over to Fenagh to see Gran. You know I'm off tomorrow and she's going to make me some of her soda bread to bring back to New York."

"What's to stop you from bringing him into town before you go to see your grandmother? It's not P.J.'s fault that ould ignorant Garda had it in for him. Imagine saying Pa Joe was footless when he only had a few on him."

"You're right, Mam. Sure, didn't the judge like me? Any time I was up before him for driving too fast, he only cautioned me. If it wasn't for that bollocks of a Garda, I'd still be driving."

Half an hour later Dermot dropped his brother off at the bookie's office and went about his business. It was later that same night when he got a call from a drunken P.J. saying he needed a lift home from Prior's pub. His horse had come in at twenty to one and he'd been at the trough all day.

Walking in through the pub door the eldest brother was greeted by,

"There you are, Dermot, you'll have one, won't ya?"

"No, no, I'm fine, P.J. Sure, I'll only be home and I have to be off to the airport. You know the car has to be given back before I get my flight." Dermot turned his head towards the door ready to go and saw Niamh Golden come in. "Ah, sure, a coffee wouldn't do me any harm," he said dropping his car keys on the counter.

The bank bailout was the main topic of the conversation. Old Hugh Cullen, so curled up over his pint at the end of the bar that it looked like he was lying across the counter, said it was all Bertie Ahern's fault.

"Sure you don't have to be a genius to know that, Hugh."

"Yeses are missing the point. That fellow was bringing trouble on us all when he let his cronies build a road through the Hill of Tara. There are things you do and there are things you don't do."

"Now are you are telling us, Hugh, that if they gave you twenty grand you wouldn't let them do whatever they wanted with your bit of land near Knockmullin?"

"Well indeed I wouldn't. The fairy hawthorn tree on my land has been there for generations. While I'm alive, no one will touch it. And, by God, that's as true as I'm standing here."

Dermot leaned over to P.J. and whispered, "Better get you home to the Mammy before the fairies come for you."

P.J. glared at his brother and told him, "Hope there's room in your case for the fairy tree along with Gran's soda bread."

He grabbed the car keys and ran out the door. Dermot went after him and saw the back of his rented Toyota heading in the direction of Knockmullin.

The shoulder of the hill was wrapped in a silvery fog. Around its neck a circle of glistening stones shone. Pale moonlit shadows seemed to drift between the boulders. P.J.'s intention had been to go into the fairy fort, break off a piece of the hawthorn tree and wave it in front of Dermot's face, but fear got the better of him. Instead he wrenched off the sat nav with the idea of hurling it into the ring of stones. P.J. leapt out of the car and pounded up the hill. Shivers ran down his spine as the low murmuring of hunting horns and barking hounds replaced the thud his boots had been making on the dry grass. He stopped; the sound stopped too. He turned around and tried to run down the hill. His ankle was grabbed and held by snarled fingers, thick as tree roots. Struggling to break free, he fell flat on his face. A deadly trembling seized him as the earth plunged beneath his body. He seemed to be falling through a trap door that had opened up underneath him. The scream that rose to his throat stopped as dreamy harp music lulled him to peace. A golden haze of floating bodies surrounded him, aiding him to land smoothly. He was enchanted as the Otherworld of the Sedhe unfolded before his stunned eyes.

A translucent Irish landscape, beautified by a thousand times, greeted his awed eyes and rendered him speechless. Tentatively he stretched out his hand to touch the air before him, half expecting his finger to dip into it, causing ripples to extend through it glimmering surface. An azure mantle, embellished with glistening clouds sparkled behind rolling hills of eighty shades of glittering green. A twinkling diamond chain of shining water flowing through the woodlands caught his gaze, but a sweet voice in his head told him to turn around. He beheld the most beautiful creature gliding towards him on milk-white feet. "My name is Emer," he heard in his mind as her emerald green eyes looked lovingly into his. She told him, "I love you," without speaking any words. Then, without knowing how, they were seated at a banquet, set on a golden table under a canopy of leafy branches. The trunks of magnificent oaks, beeches, cedars, and yews acted as the walls of this celestial hall, while the floor was carpeted by thousands of flowers of every hue and scent. P.J. realised that the petals weren't crushed by his bare feet but sprung back up again after he had stepped on them.

He was as naked as the precious pearly-skinned girl holding his hand. "With all the sins I have on me," he thought, "how the hell did I get to heaven without passing through purgatory?"

Giggles echoed in his head, so charmingly sexy that he found his mouth on Emer's lips, tenderly kissing the angel beside him. "That Oisín was an awful eejit altogether. How did he leave Niamh in Tír na Óg. I'd say there must have been a bit of a queer in him, 'cos I'm telling you, Emer, not even the Mammy is going to make me leave you."

Emer handed him the mead that she had been sipping. P.J. downed it as if it were a pint of stout, thinking "Jasus! That's awful sweet, like something the ould ones would be drinking at a wake."

Emer's soft voice whispered that her body, tasting of honey, awaited to be savoured. She wanted to know what he meant by "the ould ones" as there was no one old in their world of eternal youth and beauty. P.J. was sorry he had opened his thoughts. He kissed her mouth, hoping to shut her up and get down to business. The scene around them changed. They were lying on satin-smooth sand on the shores of a lake, aromas of a thousand flowers filling the air, a cool breeze swaying, caressing their bodies. P.J. didn't feel at ease. Was he doing what came naturally to a hot-blooded Irish man or was she in his head, directing his every move? Sitting astride him, hands gripping and pulling his blond hair, her body rose and fell in wild movements. Before he could stop himself, thoughts of horses pounding the turf came to his mind. Afterwards, to please him, now knowing he was interested in horses, they floated to the races.

When the first race started, P.J. was perplexed. A bay colt with a distinctive white blaze was galloping ahead of all the other horses. "As sure as my name is Patrick Joseph McCool those hind quarters belong to Shergar."

Emer insisted that the horse wasn't Shergar. P.J. glared at her, his thoughts hopping against the walls of his mind. "It's Shergar, I'm telling you." Leitrim man that he was, he had grown up with the legend of the kidnapped horse. The Aga Khan, owner of the stallion, was as surprised as the rest of Ireland when the great racing horse was taken, allegedly by the I.R.A., on a foggy February evening in 1983. The Gardaí combed Co. Leitrim looking for the stud. Now P.J. knew why they had never found him: the fairies had him all along.

"By dad, yeses are going to pay for all the trouble the Gardaí gave my poor father." His fists were up, swiping at anyone who was within his reach but the lack of gravity was making him reel and miss his punches. "They always thought my ould fellow had something to do with the disappearance of Shergar. They even dug up all the spuds in the back garden looking for the corpse. They were the best potatoes we ever grew. By Jasus, I'll kill the lot of yous."

Laughter filled his head. They were amused. "Oisín was right to leave this damned place. When I find the door, I'm out of here, too." Emer held his hand to calm him. She explained that they were laughing because the horse was a foal of Shergar.

"Foal, my arse. He never sired anything that won a race. If horses could be T.D.s, his offspring would have been in The Dail the night of the bank blanket guarantee." He started to stagger as the word "changeling" was pelted at him from every side. At last he understood.

"Our babies aren't enough, you take our good horses, too, and leave changelings in their place, ye whores."

Emer knew P.J. couldn't stay. She would have to kiss his smooth forehead and suck out his soul. This beautiful Milesian, like his ancestors before him, would be expelled from The Plains of Joy. His forefathers, the Fir Bolg, had been allowed to live in the magical Land of Plenty but their quarrelsome nature got the better of them and they were expelled. Even after being defeated, they turned the truth around. According to their leaders and their bards it was they, the Fir Bolg, who won the battle and imprisoned the Tuatha De Danaan in the mountains. When the Sedhe ventured out into the Milesian world, they could see that lies were still spun as truth.

Half an hour later, Dermot arrived in Niamh Golden's car. It was nearly dawn before they eventually found P.J. asleep at the bottom of the hill, the sat nav gripped tightly in his hand. They managed to get him home to bed and Dermot fixed the sat nav back on his rented car before driving to Knock Airport.

The next day, at one o'clock, P.J.'s mother was knocking loudly on his bedroom door.

"Pa Joe, come on, get up. Didn't you want to go to Enniskillen to buy some clothes?"

Her son opened his eyes and said, "Rise head and back from mattress, swing legs to floor, put weight on legs. Stand, go to door, open it."

P.J. passed his mother without looking at her and went to the bathroom door saying, "Walk for four seconds, stop in front of door, open it. Enter, walk in straight line for two seconds. Stop in front of toilet, lift up seat. Hold apparatus with right hand. Point at toilet. Shoot flow into bowl. No drop should fall on floor. Flush. Go to hand basin. Place hand on tap and turn.........."

"Pa Joe - stop your nonsense. Come on, that's a good lad."

At Shannon airport two French tourists were driving the Toyota Dermot had left at Avis Rent a Car. They typed in Swanlinbar. The sat nav started to give them directions.

"Well, first of all, yous should stop at the pub that's on the outside of Knock, they serve a great pint of Guinness there. Keep away from The Shrine: there's only rosary beads and holy water on sale in that place. Then go on for 25 km to Ballyhaunis. It's an awful town if there's a cattle mart on. You can't move an inch with the farmers and their trailers all over the place. When yous get out of it, go straight on in the direction of Carrick on Shannon. If yous see an ould stone house with a modern roof on it, yous have gone too far. Turn back to the crossroad. Take the turning on the right. If there's a big house with a fence around it, that's the right road. But make sure yous don't go anywhere near that house. It belongs to a retired teacher - he's the meanest yoke in the whole country. He had a few mangy hens and do you know what? He used to eat the potatoes with the skins on, so he wouldn't have to give the skins to the poor hens - a meaner man you never met in your life. Sure, didn't the hens die to get away from him? I'd advise yous against going to Sligo 'cos........."

The husband looked at the wife in bewilderment as the sat nav said that when they passed the house with a rusty plough in the garden, they were near Ballinamore. The voice boasted that it had spent a night with the wife. It explained how it hurt its foot on the plough jumping out the window when the husband had returned sooner than expected.

"Pierre, this sat nav is crazy. Turn it off. We will find our way by looking at the map."

Sammy

MARIETTE CONNOR

Sammy Smith pushed my dad's heavy grass cutter across our front lawn. I looked on admiringly as his bronzed arms trundled the battered lawnmower with rhythmic precision. Starting at the outside he made decreasing rectangles until, with just one short sweep, the last pieces of grass were swallowed up into the machine. He waved to me as he wheeled the mower back to the shed, to be emptied, its innards cleaned and the last hopper of grass deposited on the compost heap at the bottom of the garden.

"Nice man," Dad said, standing beside me at the kitchen window.

"He's a gypsy?" I asked.

"True Romany. Lots of them called Smith. Something to do with blacksmiths."

"Does he live in Haydon's Wood?"

"Yeah, with his mother, Rosanna. Used to tell fortunes. She must be nearly ninety by now. Sammy is well into his sixties."

Thoughts of Sammy and his fortune-telling mother were soon superseded at our Saturday lunch table by talk of the petrol strike, which was nearly a week old.

"I queued for almost three hours this morning," my mother complained, "and only got a half fill for my tank."

"Well, I'm off to Haydon's Wood this evening," said Dad. "Sammy told me he has all the time in the world to queue and has amassed a fair few cans of the stuff. I'm to go to the caravan about ten o'clock."

"Ten? That's a bit late," my mother said, as she cleared the dishes from the table. Dad smiled again and laid his forefinger along the side of his nose. "Pays to be in the know."

During the rest of the afternoon, I thought about Dad's relationship with the Gypsy Smiths. As long as I could remember, Sammy had been coming to do the heavy work in our garden. His mother's fortune-telling days were long over but I well knew the old blue painted caravan squatting by the side of the lane that always had something for sale on the table outside. In winter, sprays of red-berried holly stuck in an enamel jug - tuppence a spray, the cardboard notice held in place by a large stone. Early spring and pussy willow replaced the holly. Pretty bunches of primrose were threepence. With each season Rosanna's table reflected the changes. My mother was always keen on the blackberries, sloes and elderberries. Her prize winning jams and preserves were due to the initial hard work of the Gypsy Smiths.

I had never been inside the caravan but heard about it from Dad. It was small but spotlessly clean and crowded with beautiful pieces of cranberry glass and old Mason Ironstone jugs and dishes. There was a comfy old chair pulled up in front of a black stove whose long chimney poked through the roof. A single bed at the far end of the van was covered by a patchwork quilt. "Sammy's bed", Rosanna told Dad. "I sleep in the chair". Even indoors, Rosanna wore a faded black hat pulled down well over her ears, wisps of grey hair forever escaping from the confines of a bun. Piercing black eyes and a hooked nose gave her face a rather intimidating look, but her smile of yellowed and gold teeth was surprisingly sweet. She spoke in a cultured voice that belied her status and came as a shock to strangers. I had heard rumours in the village that Haydon's Wood had been bought for development and wondered what the Smiths would do if this happened.

Fifteen minutes short of the hour, I saw Dad get into his *Ford Popular* and head off in the direction of Haydon's Wood. Less than thirty minutes later, he was back.

"That was quick," my mother said. "How about a cuppa?"

"Cuppa be blowed - give me a brandy…a large one." Dad slumped into a chair beside the cooker. "You'll never believe it."

"Well, not if you don't tell us," my mother said, handing him a fairly full glass.

Dad's story will go down in the annals of our family history and still brings a rather bemused expression to his face in the telling. It was just on ten o'clock when he got to the caravan. Rosanna came to the half-door and, leaning out, called to him.

"Go into the clearing beyond, Sam is waiting for you." And waiting he was, sitting in the centre of the hollow, a lovely wood fire blazing away, the inevitable Woodbine in the side of his mouth and surrounded on all sides by a collection of plastic and tin cans…all full of petrol. I think Dad was ashamed at this point in the story. He called out to Sammy.

"Get the hell out of there!" even as he himself was making for the laneway and safety.

We heard later that Sam rescued the cans of fuel and Dad did, eventually, get a couple of them. Nothing more was said about the incident and, for a few months, life resumed the usual quiet routine that was Irish village life in 1950.

One evening, late in October, we had an unexpected visit from Sammy. He spoke quietly to Dad who then left with him, heading to Haydon's Wood. It was several hours before Dad returned and told Mam and me what had happened. Rosanna had died peacefully in her sleep. Sammy was heartbroken but had called on my father - who he had considered a true friend - to visit her one last time. Romanies from another village, probably relations, had arrived and were standing around in groups. They had prepared Rosanna for her last journey.

"She looked like a young girl," Dad told us. "Beautifully dressed in Romany costume, gold earrings and bracelets and lying in an oak coffin." This had been made many years ago by Sammy on her instructions. Dad made to go near the coffin and thought to kiss her forehead in farewell but was stopped immediately by Sammy. "Best not to touch her," he said. Apparently, that beautiful porcelain skin came at a price.

We had a fire that night in Haydon's Wood - not the petrol exploding kind. This one was the blaze of a blue caravan, complete with cranberry glass, Mason Ironstone and oak coffin with Rosanna.

"Tradition," Dad said later.

Sammy was moved to a small Council flat and lasted less than a year. So, no more gardening, no more berry picking or fortune telling. Only memories remain.

A Short Walk in Tall Grass

IAN BUTLER

It had been an indifferent summer, which had exploded at the end into a scorching, blinding heat-wave, lasting just over two weeks, cloudless and bursting with bright eye-watering sunlight. It was just long enough to remind people of what real summers should be like.

I had wandered back to Wiltshire to begin the mournful process of saying goodbye to my dying stepmother. I took a look at my old haunts to remind me of the happier times in my childhood. The gentle breeze reminded me of the first breeze felt after the huge heat-wave of my childhood. It was unprecedented, with days and weeks of constant sun unsullied by cloud or rain. As I walked to my old house, I began to see the images of my youth.

Behind my old housing estate, down the little lane, lay the steps that lead down to the river. Not a very large or impressive river, but its meanderings are as constant as the turning of the earth and the rising of the sun and that gentle burble has been heard for many a year. Following the path, complete with stinging nettles, couch grass and docks, I walked alone in my thoughts and dreams. Stopping at the top of the very small crest I looked down to the river and saw the iron bar, which spans it - part of the remnants of a watermill long since departed. Flooded with memories, I marvelled at how small it all seemed and how different from my own mental picture formed so very long ago.

Closing my eyes, I saw myself as a boy crossing the bar like a tightrope walker oblivious to the torrent beneath or the shouts of my mates cajoling me to go faster. I looked at the thinness of the metal bar and wondered to myself about the sense of immortality that children have I stifled a momentary impulse to cross as, forty years on, discretion was the better part of valour.

Retracing my steps I looked out on the river from a clearing that led out to the water's edge. As a kid I fished with worms here and caught nothing,

147

played kiss-chase and caught no-one and, as a young man, searched for answers and found not one. Along the bank the huge tree remained, with the hanging remnants of the rope that acted as a swing to generations of youngsters. I didn't know how it got there but one summer's day when I and the rest of my crowd had assembled to play, the rope was there. It took two minutes for my friend Jonathan to get it and pull it to the bank and soon all of us were bumping and hustling for a swing out over the river.

We weren't meant to do it but who would know? All day long kids were propelled on the improvised swing at great speed, clutching the rope for dear life. Screams of laughter, joy, exhilaration and terror met the ears of sullen lovers walking by trying to steal a few moments away from prying eyes.

All that baking summer clothes were dispensed with as kids arrived at the river, ready to splash around, dash around, muck around and run around. Their parents knew nothing: our gang swore terrible oaths of blood curdling terror to the first one to split and tell their folks. Wet clothes were explained away by reference to the paddling pool in the park or water pistol fights or any old tosh, rather than let the parents in on the secret. One boy bought matches and a fire was lit, sweets were bought and pop was guzzled by the gallon.

Every day was different and battles were fought, princesses rescued and other games invented, but "pirates" was the favourite. Like a game of chase, the pirates would catch everyone they could but if someone could swing on the rope, that released the prisoners. Hours were whiled away in this and other pursuits, until nightingales began their chorus and brothers and sisters were despatched to find missing children and bring them home for tea. That meal gobbled, a few hardy souls would come back for a bit of fishing or tree climbing or just looking for the occasional trout rising, before the setting sun would reluctantly call them home.

I stood there for what seemed hours, deep in thought with a small tear in my eye, thinking of my children and their world. Then I pitied them for only having the borrowed imaginings of TV and the Playstation, and walked a little further. Remembering later forays to the river, the images come flooding back: sneaking my first cigarette from Father's navy ration and the subsequent bout of nicotine-induced vomiting bringing gales of

148

laughter. My first taste of beer. We had all clubbed together to buy a Watney's Party Four, smuggled out a can opener and sipped the warm bitter brew, imagining it to be nectar rather than the horror that it actually was.

Walking quicker as the gentle breeze mocked my sentimentality, the scudding clouds looking disapprovingly at my rosy tinted view and I took one final look at the river. It moved snake-like through my vision, coming from somewhere and forever going somewhere else. Closing my eyes all that could be heard was the immature laughing, larking, shouting and fun-induced hysteria emanating from a group of lads long since departed, having left their happy sounds here since 1976.

The Player Who Couldn't Score

WAYNE HARDMAN

Sport may have been played less ferociously in the past. In the 1950s Ice Hockey in North America featured a large number of first generation Irish players: it's played on ice but its cut and thrust was similar to the hurling that they had left behind.

A feisty young Irish player called Eddie Convey had started playing for the New York Americans in the National Hockey League. Eddie was up from the minors and keen to prove himself but hadn't scored many goals for the Americans and was in danger of being shipped back to the minors unless his fortunes changed, and fast.

However, Convey had a couple of Irish buddies who played defence for the Toronto Maple Leafs - King Clancy and Charlie Conacher. When they discovered Eddie had difficulties they decided to give him some help. King came up with the idea and talked it over with Charlie saying, "When we play the Americans next we should build up a two or three goal lead. Then we'll let Eddie come into our zone. You miss him with a check and I'll stumble and fall to the ice. That should leave Eddie with a perfect opening to skate in and score a goal."

Sure enough, when the game was played the Leafs were ahead in the contest by three goals to nil when Eddie zipped around Charlie and flew past the stumbling King. Toronto's goalkeeper Turk Broda was also part of the plan: Turk gave Eddie half the net to score in. Not only did Eddie not score he missed the net completely.

The miss left King, Charlie and Turk dumbfounded but they decided to give Eddie a second chance.

A few minutes later Eddie picked up the puck in his own zone and skated through the centre ice area gathering speed. He flew past the Leafs blue line leaving both Charlie and King in his wake like statues.

Turk gave Eddie even more open net to shoot at - but did he score? This time Eddie took a wicket wrist shot with all his strength and let fly. The puck hit Turk square in the Adam's apple, which was more difficult than scoring. The gasping goalie looked up from the ice in a blur of disbelief. It was easier to score than hit him under the chin.

That was it. Charlie, King, and the gagging Turk agreed. "That's enough charity tonight."

"When he comes down again let's cut his legs out from under him," said King.

And that's what they did as charity was put in the bin for the rest of the night, along with Eddie's short-lived NHL career.

Corpse

DERMOT MAGUIRE

Jody and his father had moved from the kitchen onto the low bench in the narrow hallway, waiting their turn to go into the lower room where the body of their neighbour, Big Arthur, lay in the open coffin. Jody had never seen a person dead. He had seen dead pigs, and a calf that died of red water, and their cat that was killed by the bread van. He remembered, too, the budgie his cousin in town had and how quickly his legs stiffened after he died. He wondered if Big Arthur's legs were stiff like that yet. He wondered if his eyes would be open, the way the dead calf's were. He wondered if his mouth might be open the way a dead pig's sometimes was. He was fearful how Big Arthur might look; hoped and hoped that his wild, dark eyes would be closed. He was too afraid to ask his father if they would be; too afraid to ask his father or anybody about a dead person.

Jody was scared but he was curious, too. The priest had told them how the eyes mirrored the soul and how their faces reflected their goodness or their badness. This was what worried Jody: he knew that Big Arthur had lived a bad life - he had always been drinking and fighting and cursing and he had been bad to his animals. He had often heard Big Arthur, with his own two ears, shouting and cursing and whacking at his cows and he'd heard how he shot his spaniel dog dead because he wouldn't retrieve a duck from the lough. Jody had often run by his house to avoid him, and whenever Big Arthur passed him on the road his eyes were wild and blood-shot and all he would say in his deep, hoarse drawl was, 'Booy!'

One day Big Arthur was in his father's house getting tea, after he had helped to pull a calf from a cow. It was the first time he had seen him up close: his thick moustache had dirty yellow streaks in it and was clogged up with green snot. He had big hairy hands and dirty finger nails. His mother said that you could grow potatoes in them. That was the day he noticed that one of his eyes was crooked. And the smell of him: they said he slept with his dog and the last time he had a bath was the time he fell

152

into the back river trying to get a cow out of it. Big Arthur's voice was loud and so was his laugh but Jody did not think it was a friendly laugh. All these things were piling up in his head as he waited beside his father on the bench.

He could hear the babble of voices up in the kitchen where the smoke of pipes and cigarettes floated out into the hall and hung there. Then Mrs McCarney, from out the road, came round with tea and biscuits on a tray.

"Poor Arthur," she said quietly, "he never gave himself much of a chance, did he?"

"That's right. That's right enough," his father said, and said no more. Jody noticed how most of the people in the house were old. Every now and then he would hear a man's voice above the rest, saying, "That is a fact," or "That's the God's truth." He recognised Jemmy Corr's laugh a few times and was surprised that people were laughing at all. Nobody seemed to be talking much about Big Arthur. It did not sound like they were mourning.

Now he and his father were at the head of the queue. He could see the lower half of the shiny, brown coffin. He could see a candle flickering. There was lino on the floor of the coffin room with brown squares and sky blue diamonds inside them: the same colours as the rings around the big mugs on Arthur's dresser. Big Arthur was dead and he was going into the brown earth below the blue sky. The squares did not touch each other and the space between them was light grey. The lino was badly worn around the doorway, the squares and diamonds smudged and worn into fragments of blue and brown, like scattered pieces of jig-saw. He wondered if Arthur would look worn out like the lino, if all the badness would show in his face. He wondered again and again if those big wild eyes of his would be open. He got more and more uneasy but more and more curious, too.

Then it was their turn. A stranger woman ushered them into the coffin room. He was barely tall enough to see fully into the coffin. There was so much white cloth. Then he saw Big Arthur's hands with rosary beads tangled around his fingers and he could see the top of his nose. Then he saw that his eyes were closed. Closed! Thank God. Relief poured over him. He was astonished by all the white cloth and especially the whiteness of Big Arthur's face and hands. Then he felt something approaching betrayal.

He had been denied the horrible face that he had expected: Arthur alive had never looked like this. There he was; clean and calm, his thick, dirty moustache trimmed to insignificance, his pale, scrubbed hands accepting the sparkling rosary beads. He has been shaved clean - the way Billy Winters shaved the dead pigs. The shock then turned to confusion and bewilderment. Why had the priest said such things? Why had he been so sure?

Then Jody felt a sense of shame creeping over him: shame that he had judged somebody in this way; shame that he had felt such things about poor Big Arthur, but relieved to the bottom of his soul that those wild, dark eyes were closed to his.

Friends Reunited

ANTHONY VINEY

Julian Pertwee didn't like being called a nonce. *Paedophile* carried more substance, its Greek origins celebrating antiquity.

Perpetrator was better still, recognising Julian's forward planning, precision, and achievement. But *nonce!* Ah well, last day in the Scrubs. By this time tomorrow, his stinking cell and grubby companions would be consigned to memory. Julian stroked his neatly trimmed beard and pulled in a heavy paunch as he settled down to the last supper. He fingered the plastic cutlery and stared earnestly at Barry Pyke. Barely into his thirties, Pyke's skin was heavily pockmarked, and his alopecia well advanced. They shared a solitary table at the far end of the prison canteen.

There was nothing to distinguish this section of the dining area, and there was no need to signal that their places had been reserved: as every con in the block knew, *this* table was strictly set aside for the nonces.

"Hard day then, Julie? You'd think they would have brought out the best china."

Julian was used to Pyke's relentless sarcasm. They had shared a cell during the first year of his confinement, only suffering an unwelcome separation when the Governor deemed their friendship was more than benign. But twelve months had been long enough to cement their alliance.

For Julian, an apprenticeship of sorts. For Pyke, a chance to demonstrate to his student the tricks of the trade. And today, Pyke reasoned, was an opportunity for his star pupil to learn a final lesson.

"Julian, my dear, what you have to remember, is always cover your tracks. Never - I say never - use your own PC. And don't believe that bull about encryption: the forensic boys can turn up anything on your hard drive."

"So what are you saying, Pykey? No more fun online?"

"Not quite, Julian. Just don't take the piss. If you use your own equipment the old Bill can track you - and any messages and photos - right

155

back to your I.P. address, and confiscate your gear. Give them a chance to take a good old nosey and then have you bang to rights."

Julian pushed a scoop of mashed potato to the side of his plate. He examined the unsavoury globule of mucus nestling between a leaf of boiled cabbage and a hardening pork chop. He wondered whether the spittle had been issued by a warden or one of the old lags.

"Julian - are you listening? All I'm saying is that you can send the pretty little things whatever you want. Just don't use your own computer and stay on the move. Keep 'em guessing."

Tracey Fletcher stared, once again, at her reflection in the bedroom mirror. Weighing in at six stone ten, she boasted a triumphant size zero. She was frustrated, nails bitten down to the quick, and furious that no new messages had hit her post wall. Why hadn't Steve sent her another photo? She'd even adjusted the privacy settings to low to demonstrate that, for Steve, her Facebook site was open for business. A virtual love affair, conducted online and at high speed, it had lifted her spirits as she approached her fifteenth birthday. But she wanted more.

Steve had impressed her. It wasn't just that first photo - his cheeky grin as he larked about with his mates on the football pitch - it was more than that. Steve was different. Special.

"Tracey, I feel like I've known you for years".

"Tracey ....love you in that top. Where did you get it?"

"Tracey .... that last pic. You're driving me crazy."

"Tracey .... when can we meet?"

Enjoying the extended opening hours at the public library, Julian logged off his Facebook account. He tugged gently at the grey hairs making a discreet exit from his nostrils and ran his fingers along the cover of the battered school exercise book he'd discovered under the seat on the bus. It said *Tracey Fletcher. Form 5.*

Only a week out of prison, and Julian had made a new friend. "Here's hoping!"

"Goddard ... glad you could make it."

WPC Penelope Goddard, fresh from cadet school, was keen to impress. She knew she was still on probation, untested and unproven: this was her first chance to make her mark and help nail a sex offender. She eyed the fading coffee stain on the front of Detective Inspector Morrow's creased shirt. "Could do with a tidy up," she thought.

"Right, ladies and gentlemen," said Morrow, "let's see what we've got. Are you keeping up with this, Goddard?"

Penelope heard a suppressed snigger from the back of the room.

"This man calling himself *Steve*," Morrow continued, "he's always on the move. It's a job keeping up with him. We've tracked him down to internet cafes in Brixton, Peckham and Lewisham. The last location we have was posting messages in Southall."

Penelope looked towards the wall chart - a spider's web of marker pen reaching south. She'd expected Steve to make a foray into the suburbs, and had been surprised at his latest move west, into Southall. She'd hoped that Inspector Morrow would have brought a forensic psychiatrist for the strategy meeting to offer a psychological profile but the Inspector's approach remained decidedly low tech.

"Yesterday," he exclaimed, "we had a lucky break. A call from a Mrs Fletcher who's been checking her daughter's messages and photos on Facebook and went ape when she saw what was being exchanged."

Morrow flicked a few specs of dandruff from his collar and continued. "It's time we got more proactive. Set up a little meeting with this man calling himself Steve. And that, Miss Goddard, is where *you* come in."

Penelope shivered as she stood at the entrance of Southall train station. A slow drizzle had left grey streaks on her white socks. She felt claustrophobic inside the maroon school uniform that Inspector Morrow had procured for her.

"Suits you, Penelope," he'd whispered furtively.

"Dirty bastard," she'd thought.

She nodded towards the two plain-clothed officers lounging in an unmarked vehicle opposite the station and thought, "How much longer?"

Julian popped another *Fisherman's Friend* into his mouth. "Must keep the breath nice and sweet." Standing near the ticket kiosk he peered at Penelope's well-polished black shoes. "They'll make a tasty keepsake," he told himself. "Something to cherish."

He had his introduction well rehearsed. "It's Tracey, isn't it? I'm Steve's dad. Sorry, he's stuck at home – he pulled a muscle playing football, so he asked me to give you a lift. If that's OK. It'll only take ten minutes."

A simple if audacious strategy, Julian calculated, but one that had worked before.

"Well, if it ain't Penelope Goddard - what are you doing in that outfit?"

It took a moment for Penelope to recognise Paul in his police uniform. Over a year ago they'd exchanged more than kisses at the cadet graduation party. "Christ, Paul, this isn't a good time. I'm on a shout, you know, undercover. Call me later tonight - after seven."

Draining his second cappuccino, Julian checked his watch. Seven fifteen. He smeared the froth from his beard and logged on. A shot in the dark perhaps, but he had picked up the young officer's name. And her friend's name too: Paul.

Sweet.

He entered his password and moved the cursor towards *I want to be your friend.*

"Here's hoping!"

Penelope knew she had blown it. What was she thinking? Couldn't she just have ignored Paul and focused on the job in hand? She glanced at the tangle of socks, shoes, blazer and skirt lying forlornly in the corner and considered her future: a long spell in uniform branch seemed inevitable.

Resting her Bacardi on the placemat next to the computer, Penelope began to search for recent activity on her Facebook account. Her privacy settings had always been locked to maximum; she didn't care for unpleasant surprises. But there, on the screen, she was being asked whether she wanted to 'Add a Friend'.

"Hi Penelope, it's Paul."

158

Penelope took another sip of Bacardi.

"Sorry about earlier. Hope you're OK."

It had been a long day. Her fingers hovered uncertainly over the mouse.

"When can we meet?"

Two choices: accept or decline…. "Oh, what the hell…"

Changing Places, Changing Faces

TONY BRADY

When a person you meet for the first time says their occupation is *furnelling* your curiosity is stimulated. Carlos was a *furneller*: he would tell me later what this involved. He was a West Indian in his thirties, with a friendly but slightly battered face, and had become detached from his roots and his community, ending up homeless before I helped him move into his resettlement bed-sitter in Hoxton.

In the 1980s it was a rundown area where many large family houses had been converted to small upholstery and furniture workshops, with poverty the predominant influence since the nineteenth century: Charles Dickens had drawn extensively on its living conditions as graphic background to his novel *Oliver Twist*. Carlos had chosen this area because the factory he worked in was here and his friend Georgina planned to move in nearby. At that time developers and estate agents were talking up the area as being "on a cusp." The area was changing, as a letter writer to The Hackney Gazette put it: "The Nigels and the Pamelas are arriving on a tide of builder's skips."

The whole area changed rapidly as artists moved in: Rachel Whitereade, Tracy Emin, Damien Hirst, and Gilbert and George all set up studios, and small art galleries opened. The writer Martin Amis came and was inspired to write a best-selling novel: *London Fields*. For Carlos and his friend this *nouveau bohemia* would easily accommodate their unusual proclivities: here they could safely put another face on their relationship.

Carlos told me about furnelling: it involves the stripping of animal skins and stroking the fur in one direction to match it for sewing into garments. He showed me a few examples in his wardrobe, where I also noticed a lot of women's clothes. I thought they must have been Georgina's, who I hadn't yet met.

Some years later I was in the area, and decided to call in and see Carlos. The area had changed a lot, and I sat in a new wine bar studying an artist's advertisement above the bar, which featured a photo of a fur-coated dancer called Carla Candida who was a regular performer in a nearby pub-cum-restaurant-cum-disco.

At Carlos's flat the door was opened by a stranger who, despite a bushy moustache, was a woman dressed as a man. "I'm George - it's my wife that you must be after," he said, as I followed him into the flat.

Before I had time to take in the surroundings a perfectly made-up woman in a mini-skirt approached and firmly planted a lipstick-tasting kiss on my lips. I looked directly into her face and took in the fluttering false eyelashes, the carefully applied mascara, the delicately rouged cheeks, the deceptive wig, the striking ear rings. I felt a bosom pressed to my palpitating chest and detected a hint of Chanel No 5. Resistance was futile.

Carlos had become Carla. I was de-clutched and invited to tea, which was efficiently provided by his "husband." An amusing hour or so passed but I had to decline their invitation to attend that evening's performance in the *Queen's Arms*.

Sir Augustus Mortimer's Secret

IAN BUTLER

Sir Augustus always kept a strict routine. He believed in order and equilibrium. After a lifetime of service to the London and Metropole Bank, he had replaced his working regimen with his retirement regimen.

Every morning he was wakened by his manservant, Snettings, at 7.30 sharp. He would bathe and trim his beard, of which he was inordinately proud. He considered himself a patriot and his beard was fashioned on that of the King's. After his toilet, he would be served his breakfast, which always consisted of oatmeal, followed by a kipper.

His breakfast completed, Mortimer would read his correspondence with his first cigarette of the day and quietly smile or explode with impotent fury depending on what his sister Agnes had written about their nephew, or what his trainer had written about his stable of race horses. He received their letters every morning.

Today, his trainer had submitted a most satisfactory report, but Agnes had tidings of a most disturbing kind: his nephew was in trouble again. Agnes' letter conveyed the very disappointing news that their nephew was due in court today and that together they must begin to arrest his appalling behaviour.

His nephew was a complete wastrel, spoilt by indulgence from his now dearly departed sister Doris and with only Mortimer and Agnes to offer him any type of guidance.

Fuming, he rang the bell for his butler. "Ah, Snettings, send a telegram to my nephew's manservant. Please ensure that he is delivered here as soon as possible after his visit to the Beak this morning."

Snettings, familiar with Mr Mortimer's nephew, made the appropriate grimace, before reminding Sir Augustus of his diary for the day.

"You will remember, Sir, that you have an appointment with a writer this afternoon, the one you commissioned to write about your years at the London and Metropole Bank."

162

"Blast," exploded Mortimer, his temper getting the better of him before he had an idea. His nephew might profit from being exposed to this writer, especially as he would be writing about his rise to the top of that fine bank. And the writer would gain some assistance, and equilibrium would reign. Pleased with his wheeze, Mortimer continued unabashed.

"Let us keep both appointments, Snettings, as my nephew may at least learn something from my memoirs."

"Very good, Sir Augustus, I will make the arrangements."

His correspondence dealt with, Mortimer walked to his club - that place of peace and tranquility reserved strictly for gentlemen and he was keen, along with his fellow members, that it was kept like that. The venerable banker and his colleagues had no time for men who, for instance, drove their own motor cars or who did not read *The Times*. Examples of free thinking like that would have them instantly blackballed and exiled to institutions that would tolerate such behaviour.

He would take the first Scotch and soda of the day at his club and read his freshly ironed copy of the Times. His mood thereafter would depend on three things: his approval of the news therein, the form of his favourite racehorse *Empire Pride*, and the price of his remaining bank stock.

His horse having triumphed in a Derby trial, he thought that he could face the other news with equanimity. However, the bank stock had taken a tumble and, in the news pages, was the public revelation that his nephew was due before the Beak at a local Assizes.

His face turned puce, mirroring his current state of apoplexy but as he kept his nephew's behaviour secret from the other members he had no outlet for his fury and had to keep the explosive vapours within. This task was made more difficult by the problems at luncheon: the Cook was on holiday, and his favourite steak and kidney pudding was off. He settled for a chicken dish that he found peculiarly unpalatable and by the end of his meal Sir Augustus' mood was like an unstable volcano ready for a Krakatoa-like explosion.

Returning home via the park, the work of upsetting his equilibrium that his sister Agnes had begun that morning was completed by a street urchin who spied his fine beard and yelled, "BEAVER," at the top of his lungs. Sir

Augustus Mortimer felt even more disagreeable. When he arrived home, he was greeted by Snettings who informed him that his guest was in the drawing room, and his nephew had been fined £10 by the Beak and was on his way over.

He asked Snettings who had paid the fine. On being told that his nephew's butler had stumped up the cash, he asked for his cheque book to repay the debt.

Now harassed beyond his ability to mask his feelings, the irascible financial giant strode into his drawing room, and saw the writer sitting on the couch. After extremely short pleasantries had been observed, Mortimer strode around the room, lecturing his guest on the folly of youth and his nephew in particular.

He vented his accumulated fury and voiced his despair for the future of England and the Empire. At length he described his nephew and his cronies. His friend with the lizards, and the silly ass who fell in love with the Red revolutionary's daughter, causing a stir at Ascot. Hardly pausing for breath, he listed the scandals that included running a sweepstake on the length of each sermon at the local parish churches surrounding his sister's country pile; the theft and return of his brother-in-law's precious silver trinket was also described to the bewildered writer, along with his nephew's current exploit of knocking off a policeman's helmet - this offence committed following the failure of his college rowing team at Henley. He continued in this vein, contrasting the behaviour of his nephew with his own career at the London and Metropole. The tirade continued for nearly an hour until Snettings arrived with some tea and an announcement that Mortimer's nephew had arrived.

His nephew breezed in and, nodding to the writer, got straight to the point.

"Dearest Uncle, my exploits before the Beak this morning have left me a little short and my man has had to pay up to save me from Chokey. Could I put the bite on you till my allowance is due?"

Mortimer puffed out his considerable chest. "This will not do at all and I cannot pay without some commitment from you to assist me in my writing enterprise. Only if you consent to this I will repay your man."

164

His nephew silently groaned. However, such was the price of keeping on the right side of his uncle's pocket book that he reluctantly agreed to the miserable terms on offer.

His uncle told him, "I want you to meet this young man as he endeavours to write some memoirs and hopefully provide you with a model of how to make yourself useful."

His nephew and the writer looked at each other. Uncle asked the author, "Do you think there is enough material for a book?"

"I would say absolutely, and without a doubt, Mr Mortimer. Several books I would say."

Mortimer smiled for the first time that afternoon. "In which case I have the pleasure of introducing my nephew, Mr Bertie Wooster. Bertie, this is Mr P.G. Wodehouse, the writer."

The Boy Who Wasn't There

DIANE JARDEL

Claire chased the last soggy cornflake around in the milk with her spoon, and looked up at her mother washing her father's blue shirt on the bumpy glass in the wooden framed scrubbing board. She drank the remaining milk, holding the bowl up to her mouth like a cup as her mother turned the handle of the mangle to make the two cylinders revolve. The shirt was transformed from a soggy wet lump into what looked like a dry flattened piece of cardboard, the water steaming from it and sploshing into the deep square porcelain sink below. The rising steam covered the kitchen window hiding the trees outside. Her mother sighed, pushed her brown hair back from her forehead with a wet hand and stood up straight to rub her back. "Stop hanging around staring at me - go into the garden and pick some blackberries," she told her 5 year old daughter. She hung the shirt on a wooden clothes frame and winched it up on a pulley where it would hang to dry near the kitchen ceiling, above the coal fired boiler.

Claire climbed down from her chair, took the bowl her mother gave her and went out of the side door into the narrow passage between her flat and Malcolm and Peter's flat. She descended the concrete steps into the garden and noticed a large rusty, three wheeled bike standing under Malcolm's window. She walked around the bike; she preferred riding Peter's two-wheeled bike but she wanted to try this one out.

Last week Peter, who was ten years old, had let her ride his bike down the steep road just beyond their block of flats. She stood on the pedals because the frame was too big for her, whizzed down the hill screaming with pleasure then leapt off it at the bottom of the road because the bike's brakes didn't work. The bike crashed to the ground on its side, wheels still spinning as Claire lay on the ground laughing with joy at her amazing feat of travelling faster than she ever had before.

Compared with the daredevil skill of riding a two-wheeler, riding a three-wheeled bike would be very tame. She ran back into the flat. Her

166

mother was pouring coal into the top of the boiler from the coal scuttle; dust poured out of the small opening. "Mummy, there's a three-wheeled bike outside Peter's window. Who's is it?" she asked.

Her mummy gave a mysterious smile. "Oh, that bike. It's for Peter and Malcolm's cousin."

Claire frowned, a crease forming between her light brown eyebrows, "But Peter and Malcolm's cousin lives in Canada."

"Well, there's a cousin you haven't heard of before," her mother told her. "Where are those blackberries I asked for?"

Still puzzled, and not believing her mother, Claire went out to their garden across the grass to the blackberry bushes which grew on a wall that fell ten feet down to another garden and some garages. She reached out for each blackberry, holding the fruit gently so the overripe berries did not get squeezed into a mush, and making sure that she didn't get pricked by the thorns around the bushes.

The next day she went out to find someone to play with and saw her daddy scraping the rust off the three-wheeled bike.

"What are you doing that for?" she asked.

He looked up from his crouching position, his brown eyes smiling. "I'm helping Mr Lederman clean this bike up."

How strange, Claire thought: she had never seen her daddy helping Mr Lederman before.

Over the next few weeks the three-wheeled bike was transformed. It had been repainted a matt blue and the metalwork sparkled. Claire waited expectantly to meet this new cousin.

"What's your cousin's name?" Claire called across to Malcolm as they competed to see how high they could go on the swings.

"My cousin?" asked Malcolm.

"The one who's going to get the three-wheeled bike under your kitchen window."

"Oh, that cousin," grinned Malcolm as he pumped his legs faster to swing higher than Claire. "His name's...his name's Robin."

The day of her sixth birthday arrived. There was a home-made chocolate sponge cake on the table with a paper frill around it. Her mummy, daddy and big sister sang *Happy Birthday* to her. Claire shut her eyes, made a secret wish and blew out the candles.

"There's a surprise outside for you," announced her curly-haired sister. They all went outside to the back garden and there was the matt blue three-wheeled bike with a red bow on it and a girly saddlebag on the back.

"Surprise!" everyone shouted. "This is *your* birthday present," her dad whispered to her.

"But it's Malcolm's cousin's bike," Claire protested.

"We told you that so you wouldn't know it was your surprise present," her mother told her.

Claire looked at the bike, confused and disappointed. Why had her parents lied to her? Why had they let her get bored with the bike before they told her it was her present? Where was Malcolm's cousin? And when would she ever get a two-wheeled bike?

"Well try it out," urged her mother.

Claire climbed onto the bike and rode it between the two buildings towards the front garden. She would never think of it as her bike: it would always be the phantom cousin's three-wheeler.

Unforeseen

GORDON WILLIAMS

Madame Sophia had the gift: she could see things. Now, she saw her own reflection in the mirror as she touched up her frosted pink lipstick and the light flashed off her dangly gold earrings when she turned her head from side to side. She adjusted her brightly-patterned aquamarine silk headscarf, a colourful contrast to her all-black trousers, blouse and gold-buttoned waistcoat. Pleased with the effect, she switched off the light to leave the small room lit only by candles. The Venetian blinds were closed and the smell of jasmine drifted upwards from an incense burner on a little table in front of them. Madame sat down at one of two dark leather armchairs either side of a round table with a crystal ball and a Tarot deck on top of its purple silk cloth cover.

She read: *4.30 pm. Pamela Goodwin* from her appointments book - a late booking following a cancellation. Today's last client, thank God. She lay back in her armchair, closed her eyes and took slow, deep breaths. After the sixth breath somebody knocked at the door to her room, pushed it open and entered.

Madame Sophia opened her eyes to see a tall woman who introduced herself.

"Hello, I'm Pamela's sister. She couldn't make it today. You know how it is: unforeseen circumstances. I didn't want to waste her appointment - I know you're booked up for weeks ahead. I've heard so much about you and I thought I'd ask if I could take her place," she said, and sat down in the other armchair without waiting for an answer.

Madame Sophia was impressed by her cheek, but it hardly mattered who the woman was: a customer was a customer and twenty pounds was twenty pounds.

"Certainly," she told her new client. "What's your name?"

"Call me Helen."

"How can I help you?"

169

"Well, Pamela told me that you usually do a general reading and then you answer questions that people ask you." She pointed to the crystal ball on the table between them. "Do you use that?" she asked.

"No," the woman opposite smiled and shook her head. "It's more of an ornament – almost a joke. I don't need it."

Her client looked disappointed but told her, "I've been having some family problems recently. I want to know if they will be over soon. I want to sort things out." She looked directly across the table and continued, "That's why I'm here now."

The head in the headscarf nodded and looked back at Helen. She saw, as anybody could, a good-looking woman in her late forties. Madame Sophia had recognised her client's midnight blue Chanel handbag and Christian Louboutin mini-heels - she'd seen them in magazines – before she'd sat down. Now she saw her gold necklace and earrings: understated but expensive. The real thing. Helen had obviously looked after herself: her trim figure, dyed auburn hair and light make-up were close to perfect and she looked comfortably elegant in her navy two-piece suit.

Madame Sophia could see more than that. "You don't have any financial problems," she began, looking directly at Helen, "… your family had some land or property which was left to you rather than money. You used this to set yourself up in business…a partnership with another member of the family…you have been very successful and don't need to work anymore… you do it because you enjoy it…something to do with clothes or jewellery… accessories of some kind… your sister has had a lot of problems recently but they'll end soon…the next two years will bring her some important changes… I don't see any children of your own…you may have rather mixed feelings about that… hmm… you have some land with horses near your home. Are you a Sagittarius?"

"No, a Scorpio," her client replied.

"Ah, yes – the eyes - I should have seen it," Madame Sophia continued, surprised at her client's lack of response. Her one reply was the only feedback from her; there were no other clues if what she had told her was right or wrong. People usually said, "Yes, that's right," or, "How did you know that?" or sometimes they would tell her she was wrong. But Helen said very little and her face and body language gave nothing away.

170

Strangest of all, her aura hardly changed while she was listening: the hazy red radiance of suppressed anger permanently ensheathed her. What was she angry about?

Helen continued staring as Madame resumed. "Your mother has been ill recently...but she's getting better now, although it looks like a long-term problem... something to do with her chest or her breathing?" she looked at her client, keeping silent and hoping for some confirmation.

"She has asthma. She's always had asthma," Helen replied, but said no more.

Madame Sophia gave a short cough and continued, "She's not really been well since her husband died a few years ago... she tries to use her illness to get some attention from other members of the family, including you. Is that why you've come to see me now?"

"No. She's been like that for years. She can't manipulate me now."

Madame Sophia paused before taking a different direction. "There's a man... his face isn't clear... but he wears a suit at his work. He has his own business and he's away from home sometimes because of his work...he meets a lot of people and you..." she paused again and saw the red cloud around her client intensify: this had to be the reason. She considered her words to avoid saying what she saw, "...and you aren't always happy about the social contacts he makes when he's away from home."

"That's my husband and I suspect he's been having an affair," Helen said. Her face and voice hardly changed but her aura swirled upwards around her throat and head, its darkening redness the only clue to her client's anger.

"That's it," thought Madame Sophia. She kept her own face as expressionless as she could and asked, "Is that the family problem you mentioned?"

"Yes," was the only reply.

Madame Sophia chose her words carefully. "It looks as if there has been a relationship on an occasional basis... but it's likely to end soon... very soon. Have you asked your husband about this?"

"No, I don't need to. I know by his behaviour. I just wanted you to confirm what I believed. And you have. Are you telling me it will be over very soon?"

171

"That's what it looks like."

"Pamela told me that you were very good and she was right: everything you have told me is true. Are you sure this … this relationship will end soon?"

Madame Sophia replied, "It looks as if it has run its course… has almost ended already."

"Thank you so much," Helen told her, still expressionless. "I feel so relieved at what you have told me."

The face in the headscarf smiled, feeling relieved herself but this ended as her client pointed at the crystal ball between them and asked, "Can I look into your crystal ball for a moment?"

Madame Sophia was too surprised by this request to say "No," and watched in silence as Helen leaned forward to lift the crystal ball and its shiny black plinth to her side of the table and stare as intently at the opaque orb as she had at her.

"I can see… yes… a young girl in a country village," Helen began. "She's a Pisces. People say she has a vivid imagination but she doesn't think that. She believes she has the gift…she can see things… but she has to stop telling people what she sees because they may think that she's strange. She wants to be an actress… or a singer. She likes dressing up and showing off… she does have some talent but she doesn't have the confidence to do what her heart really wants… I see her later with two children…a boy and a girl… and when they are older she goes back to work but gets bored with it… until she does something that she's really good at…it's not acting or singing… even though she'd really love to be Madonna… no… she's involved with people, giving advice in some capacity… she's very good at what she does… she doesn't use her real name… that's Joan… or Jane… something very ordinary…and she's not an actress but she's learned how to put on a performance when she's working… and … and I can see a man… an honest, straightforward sort of man who works with his hands… he's a carpenter or builder of some sort… a Taurus… or possibly a Capricorn. He's done a lot of work on their house in the country. He's called Gerry or Geoff… I think it's Geoff… and… I can see another man… an older man, but he's not this woman's father… no…she meets him when she stays overnight in the city… she works a long way from home where

172

nobody knows her. This older man is very different to the people that this woman usually meets... he's educated and he's wealthy... and he knows his way around. He pays her attention like nobody else has ever done... and he makes her laugh... he's the only man who makes her feel as special as she thinks she is... she doesn't have to hide anything from him... but she does have to hide something from Geoff."

Helen paused to stare at a face drained of colour, with a pallor that the candlelight exaggerated and make-up couldn't conceal. Madame Sophia felt faint, too bothered to notice Helen's aura now, as she resumed her story. "She's very pleased with herself... she's been making a lot of money and everything has been going so well... but... but there's a sudden change... the older man has been found out and...it's...it's all over." Helen looked directly at Madame Sophia for a few seconds and then back at the crystal ball.

"There's something else...yes... she's driving home at night... it's a long way back to her house in the country...there's a lot of rain and spray on the road... and...and there's an ... accident..." Helen paused and slowly shook her head. "I really shouldn't say any more...it all looks...it looks most unpleasant."

She looked up again at Madame Sophia. "That's all I can see. You really should use the crystal ball more," she said as she pushed it back to the centre of the table. "You can see so much with it."

Helen picked up her Chanel handbag from the floor and asked, "How much do you charge?"

Madame Sophia was too shocked to reply at first, and only managed, "Twenty pounds," after several seconds.

Her client took a twenty pound note from somewhere inside her bag and put it on the table by the crystal ball. "You're cheaper than I thought," she told the stunned clairvoyant, standing to say, "but I'm sure it's been time and money well spent."

Madame Sophia managed, "Thank you," as her client left and barely echoed her "Goodbye."

Too upset to move from her chair, she sat thinking over what Helen had told her. How could she have known all that? Did she have the gift? She shook her head and felt her earrings jangling, sitting for a minute with her eyes closed to see if anything more came to her, but nothing did. She stood to switch on the light, blow out the candles and burning incense and, as she opened the blinds, she saw rain hitting the window in the fading November light.

Standing before the mirror, she took off her headscarf and earrings and shook her dark hair down to become Joan again. She picked up the twenty pound note and collected her belongings together in her handbag, gripping her rattling keys as she locked the door. Then she walked downstairs and out into the rain, to drive home as carefully as her shaking hands would allow.

Conquering The Shadows

DIANNE TRIMBLE

"Time for bed, children." Frances glanced up at the mahogany clock on the mantelpiece. The last Sligo-bound train was always punctual. The engineer would give one short blast of its whistle as the train left the station. Once she heard the hissing steam of its farewell she knew that it would not be long until Anthony would be home, but that train whistle would not be for more than an hour yet. She frowned and twisted the locket hanging at her neck between her thumb and forefinger. Frances could never settle when Anthony's job as a signalman on the Sligo, Leitrim & Northern Counties Railway kept him away from home in the evening.

She stood up, smoothing the creased cotton of her navy dress and set her sewing on the chair, careful to tuck the needle into the fabric.

"Will I hold the candle for you, Mammy? You'd see your sewing better," Michael, her eldest child asked, stalling for extra time.

"No, I'll manage, thank you. It's getting late. Come along now."

She hurried across the room and tugged the door handle, suppressing a shiver as the warped wood of the architrave released its grip and the draught from the hall swept past her. Michael stood up slowly, reluctant to leave the fire. His sister, Ellen, hunched next to him. He grasped her hand and pulled her to her feet. She snatched her hand away from him then bent over and pinched their younger brother who was dozing beside her. David rubbed his arm as he jumped to his feet. He scowled at Ellen who feigned innocence as she walked away. Frances tightened her lips to hide her smile.

"Don't be tormenting your brother, Ellen. Apologize, please."

"Sorry, David," Ellen said, trying to sound contrite.

Under their mother's unflinching gaze the three children filed out of the room. David bumped against the well-worn banister rail and stamped his feet on each stair as they climbed to the floor above.

"Stop that noise, David! Mrs. Mohan will be asleep. Don't you waken her. You know she can hear us through the wall," Frances admonished. *Though it's no less than that woman deserves,* she thought. *They're not bad children but she finds fault every time she meets them.*

Obeying their mother's instructions the children quickly undressed in the cold bedroom, slipped on their white cotton nightshirts and knelt to say their prayers.

"God bless Daddy, Mammy, Michael, David and all the neighbours except Mrs Mohan," Ellen concluded. Frances choked back a laugh, coughing instead. She composed her face as the children opened their eyes.

"Ellen, you must include Mrs Mohan in your prayers," Frances said.

"But she shouts at me, Mammy."

Frances gave the child a stern look then shook her head. "Well, never mind that now. Into bed with you, children. And I don't want to hear any whispering. Goodnight, my dears."

She kissed each child on the forehead then closed the door behind her as she left the room. The candle flickered in the draught as she descended the stairs. Shadows leapt around her. The hallway had not seemed so menacing when she had ushered the children up to their room a few minutes earlier. She had forgotten briefly how much she hated the dark. But, alone now, she stared straight ahead, trying not to notice the shadows lunging out of the walls. There was one just ahead that stretched up from the floor below, projecting its monstrous shape towards her. *It might be someone standing at the foot of the stairs waiting to pounce on me,* Frances thought. Her heart hammered but she willed herself to go on. A stair creaked behind her. She did not turn around, fearing she might catch sight of someone standing there, close enough to reach out and grab her.

Frances had been afraid of the dark for as long as she could remember. As a child on her family's farm she had shuddered as she carried buckets of milk to sick calves in the byre on dark winter afternoons. When she stepped from the house into the haggard the trees surrounding it threw leering shadows in her path and she would run through them, spilling milk from the bucket. Once in the byre she avoided looking into its dark corners, trying to ignore the rustlings and scrapings she heard.

In the farmhouse after darkness descended each evening she would never stray out of the reach of candlelight or the fire's glow. At bedtime she would race from the kitchen to her bedroom, sometimes stubbing her toes on the stairs in the dark, to escape the hallway's empty blackness and the floorboards' creaks and groans. In bed she would pull the blankets over her head to mute the rattling of the window pane and protect herself from the shadows that danced through it onto her bed when the moon was bright. She feared that the shadows would materialize into fairies who would snatch her from her bed.

This is silly, she thought. *I'm not a child anymore and I know the fairies want nothing from me. There's no one there. Why am I so frightened? The children are only in the room above me and another hour will see Anthony home. I'd loathe calling on her but Mrs Mohan is next door if needs be. So I've nought to fret about.*

But Frances gripped the candle tightly and hurried down the last few stairs. Bursting into the sitting room she created a rush of air that almost extinguished the candle. She stopped and waited for the flame to settle. She didn't want to find herself alone with only the fire's twisting flames to light the room. From the bedroom above she heard whispering and Ellen's giggles.

"Quiet, children. Go to sleep," she said in the sternest voice she could muster when her vocal chords were taut with fright. Frances set the candle on the table beside her chair and lifted her sewing. She strained to see the needle in the dim light, squinting as she peered at her work.

I can't see the stitches. Perhaps I will just sit here for a while, she thought. Rubbing her eyes, she set the sewing into the basket beside the chair. She leaned back but could not relax the tense muscles in her shoulders and back.

Sparks flew from a log in the fire, as it fell into the space left by the one beneath it that had crumpled and disintegrated to ash. Several sparks landed on the hearth as the log shifted. She jumped and gave a nervous laugh. *I'll sweep them away in the morning when they have cooled,* she thought, trying to distract herself.

177

Outside the wind howled. A storm had been threatening since tea time. The window panes rattled as the wind found cracks in the wood to slip through, creating a whistling noise that echoed the howling outside. Above this noise, Frances heard a sound like a cry, low at first but quickly rising. It sounded almost human. Could someone be outside in this weather? She knew she should go to the window to see if anyone was there. They would be drenched and she should invite them in to dry off at the fire. But the sound unnerved her.

What would she see if she pulled back the curtain? she wondered. What if nothing were there but the wailing continued? If the sound weren't human, then what might it be? She reached for her locket and tugged at the chain as she stared at the curtain, unable to move.

"Mammy, David says someone is calling at the window," Ellen shouted from the room above.

Frances forced herself to rise and walk to the doorway, keeping her upper body taut to stop her arms from trembling.

"It's only the wind," she said, her voice quavering. *That's surely what it is,* she thought, wanting to convince herself as much as the child. "Now, hush and go to sleep," she added, keeping her voice almost steady.

Frances paused in the doorway of the sitting room, unwilling to go back to her seat by the fire. It was comforting to hear the children above her. It was much harder to ignore the creaks and groans around her when she was on her own beside the fire.

It's only the house settling, she told herself but she avoided looking into the dark corners outside the reach of the candle or the firelight.

"Mammy, that noise makes me feel cold. Can't I come back to the fire?" Ellen asked.

Frances opened her mouth, intending to tell the child that there was nothing to fear and to insist that she close her eyes and go to sleep but she hesitated. The noise grew louder outside. Was it a cry?

Don't be silly, it's only the wind rushing through something - a crack in a fence or a broken window pane, she told herself. But, before she could change her mind, she called up the stairs, "If you're cold, come and sit by the fire for another while." She heard bangs and scurrying above and three pairs of bare feet pounding on the floorboards.

178

"But we won't make a habit of it, mind," she added, trying to sound more confident than she felt. *I'm not indulging them*, she thought. *It's a cold night and they'd be better by the fire.* She did not admit to herself that she needed their company and she might be indulging herself more than them.

The children raced down the stairs and into the sitting room. They flopped in front of the hearth, pushing and shoving as they sprawled on the rug.

Frances pulled her chair close in behind them. She kept her eyes fixed on the fire, avoiding the undulating shapes on the walls around them.

"Look at that shadow lepping," Michael said, pointing to the far corner of the room. "It's like a dog beggin' for scraps."

Ellen whimpered and pulled herself closer to her mother. "Does it bite?"

"Don't be daft, Ellen. Can't you see it's a friendly dog?" Michael said.

Frances studied the shadow. It did look like a dog. How could she have found it menacing only a few minutes ago? As she listened to the children chatting, the creaks and rustlings around them faded away until Frances ceased to notice them. The shadows took on new forms too but, like the begging dog, they were friendly ones. The children's imaginings transformed the shadows, setting her free from their power to frighten her. The wind still howled but it didn't trouble her either. It no longer sounded human, just like the wind.

"Is that someone outside, Mammy?" Ellen asked again.

"No, the wind can make lots of different sounds. That's just it blowing away the rain. It will push it far away from us before morning. Then tomorrow will be a lovely day," Frances answered. She smiled and settled back into her chair.

Jacobs' Treasure Trove

MARIETTE CONNOR

All of us have our own key to the past - something that takes us back to days when we, and the world around us, were different. I only have to open my eyes in the morning to see a small picture on my bedroom wall and I am transported back to my childhood in the forties. The picture? A short pathway through a wood and at the end is a country-style wooden gate, leading to...where? It's still a mystery. I used to spend time wondering where the gate led and what lay beyond. The picture was one of many treasures my mother, sisters, and myself received from a neighbour's shop, always known to us as Mr. Jacobs' treasure store.

There was also a Mrs. Jacobs. She was a short, plump, rosy-cheeked lady of about sixty. She sold newspapers, sweets and cigarettes and I suppose hers was the *real* shop as the name over the door read *J. Jacobs* with *Licensed to sell tobacco* in smaller print beneath. But it was the room at the back of the shop which attracted us even more than the jars of bulls' eyes, liquorice pipes and conversation lozenges which Mrs. Jacobs displayed on colourful saucers in her window.

The small room at the rear of the shop was officially used for making tea and folding up the strips of newspaper into funnels to hold sweets. Mr. Jacobs seldom appeared in the shop but was always on hand to chat and show us his treasure trove. Mother told us he was in bad health. "He does the books, makes the tea and collects things," my eldest sister, Dora, announced. She was eleven and an authority on practically everything.

There was no doubt about the collections: a long side table, an oak cupboard and some deep shelves were full of the flotsam he had collected. It covered every available space in mysterious heaps and shaky towers. Ivory paper knives, pieces of ebony and mother-of-pearl handled cutlery; ostrich feathered fans and odd bits of jewellery glinted and shone in the dark recesses of the shelves. They beckoned me, glittering like exotic mountains: a world of opulence in the greyness of 1940s Ireland. Nothing in the treasure trove had a price tag. If you wanted something, Mr. Jacobs would look at you with a twinkle in his small eyes and ask, "What do *you* think it's worth?"

It wasn't just the treasures themselves that were fascinating - it was the stories that went with them. When I pointed out one extraordinary item, I was told it was used to eat crab or lobster. A query about a silver samovar led to a long tale about the Romanovs and the mystery of Anastasia. When I was recovering from pneumonia, the doctor recommended eggs whisked in brandy and a vicious iron tonic. I refused to drink the vile potion and wasn't making much progress. Mother took me to visit the Jacobs' shop for a treat and Mr. Jacobs took me into his treasure trove. He held up a golden haired china doll dressed as a fairy. I was transfixed! There was a price to pay, however. My entry to the magic grotto after this was to force down the horrible medicine and drink down the raw egg in brandy. I had to show him the empty glass. With no school for me, I spent quite a lot of time with Mr. Jacobs. I was rewarded for my efforts with the medicine: I got to try on kid gloves, played with Chinese chessmen dressed as warlords and once, even, had my egg concoction from a real Venetian goblet.

"All good things must come to an end," my mother said, when she told us that Mr. and Mrs. Jacobs were retiring. The Jacobs could have travelled to exotic places after the war but faraway places didn't suit our friend. All he'd ever wanted was their debris, their odds and ends and the chance to say to some wide-eyed children, "What do *you* think it's worth?"

And Then There Were Two

WAYNE HARDMAN

Northern Canada is frozen solid during the winter months, and it seems to go on forever. It's so cold that your exhaling breath would freeze solid, breaking your toes if you weren't quick footed.

The Eskimos that live there know all about the dangers of the ice floes and Noni, a young Eskimo boy and his dog - a husky named Nimuk - faced the fate of many who lived and hunted on the ice. They were trapped for their third night on a passing ice floe and both Noni and his dog were getting hungrier. The two castaways were the only living things on this floating island. As the ice had broken up Noni lost virtually everything: his sled, together with all the food, his precious fur and even his knife.

He only managed to save Nimuk, his devoted husky, but even that was a miracle. Now dog and boy eyed each other suspiciously each keeping their distance. If only they had carried their new kayak. But it was his father's sledge that was Noni's main concern. How was he going to explain losing that? His other consideration was his love for the husky which was as real as the hunger and cold nights they both had endured.

Not forgetting the pain from his injured leg, which was made secure in his homemade brace constructed out of remnants that were scavenged from their equipment and their village camp some weeks ago.

The men of his village had killed their dogs when there was no food left. That thought crept fleetingly into Noni's mind. He knew that the local hunters did it without thinking or regret. He wondered if his love for his husky would overcome such an outcome. "When hungry enough one seeks whatever food there is," Noni told himself. "One of us will be eating the other."

He needed a plan - he could not kill the dog with his bare hands as Nimuk was stronger than he was, and he had no weapon. Noni thought of his makeshift leg brace and took it off his leg. He had hurt the leg a few weeks ago and had made the brace from two thin strips of steel and pieces

182

of harness. He put one of the steel strips into a crack in the ice and began to rub the other against it with firm slow strokes. This caught Nimuk's interest and the husky watched him, with eyes glowing more brightly as the passing night drifted by.

Noni worked on, trying not to remember why. The steel strip started to take shape and even had an edge to it now. When the crystal clear dawn broke Noni pulled the finished knife from the ice and thumbed its edge. The sun's glare reflected off it, blinding him for a moment.

"Here, Nimuk," called Noni softly. The husky watched the boy suspiciously. "Come here." Nimuk crept closer and Noni read fear in the husky's eyes.

He also recognised hunger and suffering in the husky's heavy breathing. He hated himself for what he had to do. The closer the suspicious Nimuk came to the boy the more Noni felt a thickening in his throat. He now saw the dog's eyes more closely and they were all full of suffering. Now - now was the time to do it!

A great sob shook Noni's body. He cursed the knife and threw the weapon as far as his weakened body would allow. He stumbled towards Nimuk and fell. The husky immediately circled him and now he was coming up from behind his fallen body. Fear shut the boy's eyes as he awaited the impending attack. Noni hoped it would be both swift and painless. Nimuk growled as he circled the young Eskimo's body, now sick with fear and completely defenceless.

Too weak to crawl away and retrieve the knife or defend himself Noni was at the husky's mercy: the dog was hungry. Nimuk circled the boy again, coming up from behind for the kill. Noni prayed for a quick end. He felt the dog's feet at his legs and its breath at his neck. A scream was building in Noni's throat as he felt the dog's tongue warm and friendly against his face. Noni opened his eyes and he cried softly putting his arm up to pull the husky's head down against his own as he passed out.

A short time later a seaplane flew in from the south. The pilot was from Canada's coastal patrol whose job was to monitor the ice floes and report their numbers and flow direction back to base. He saw the large floe and several smaller groupings. As he began to log its movement the pilot saw a flash - the sun reflected off something shiny. The pilot became curious and

183

circled the floe and picked out two dark still shapes. Or were they just mirages? His curiosity aroused, he set the plane down on the water to investigate.

Were the shapes human or just seals basking? Yes, there were two bodies there - a young boy and his husky. The boy was unconscious but just alive; the husky whined a little but was too weak to move.

The gleaming object that had caught the pilot's eye was the homemade knife discarded several yards away from the pair. The blade had stuck in the ice and was still quivering in the wind.

Cream Cookies

KEN RAMSEY

The six cream cookies were carefully placed in the white cake box. The lid was closed and sellotaped by the girl in the baker's shop. I volunteered to carry it and my brother Desmond elected to act as extra security on the walk along Bundoran Main Street and down to our holiday caravan near the beach. Bundoran is right beside the sea, and not just the sea but the Atlantic Ocean. Everything about the town was different from my home town thirty miles inland. It had a clean, seasidey, breezy smell; the daylight was brighter and the glorious red sun set far out at sea. It had its own distinct sound of distant music, muffled loudspeaker announcements and the constant mechanical buzz of the amusements. The steady tumbling crash of the Atlantic waves on the beach paced the time, day and night. My family went to Bundoran almost every year for our summer holiday. That year, the year of the cream cookies, there was my father and mother, my brother Desmond – two years younger than me – and our baby brother Ivan.

Every day during our holiday we walked the short distance from our caravan to the beach. My mother and father would sit on a rug and watch the waves tumble ashore. Desmond and I would explore every rock and pool along the beach. Sometimes we would take Ivan but mostly he would sit between my mother and father and shout at every wave coming ashore. We returned to the caravan for lunch and went back to the beach for the afternoon. If we behaved, and caused our parents no bother, Desmond and I would begin to canvass them for our reward – cream cookies – and after four or five days they always relented, so we would set off to the main street and bakery.

This year was no different until walking down the street, cookies cradled securely, we met Mrs Blair and her son Clive from home. They were in Bundoran on a church day trip. Mrs Blair was a friend of my parents. Her husband had died when Clive was a baby; he was the same age as

185

Desmond now. When my mother heard they were looking for a tea shop she insisted, after respectful protest, that Mrs Blair and Clive came to the caravan and had tea with us. Desmond and I began to grow uneasy. As we set off Desmond moved in between the cream cookies and Clive. Mrs Blair was fat and so was Clive. I was now deeply involved in mathematics.

Back in the caravan, tea and sandwiches were made and, on a plate, in pride of place in the middle of the table sat the cream cookies. Desmond and I were really miffed when we were relegated to a bunk bed because there was now no room for us at the table. We ate in silence eyeing the six cream cookies. Every year the mathematics had been the same: one for my mother, one for my father, one for Desmond, one for me and two left over. We loved cream cookies and would lick the squeezed-out cream back into the cookie, then carefully bite pieces off around the edge until there was just the centre of the bottom heaped with cream. Then, with a final flourish, we would push this piece into our mouths and chomp away until it was gone. My mother and father would offer the last two to each other; they always refused and, much to our glee, they were given to us. Now I was counting and with a sinking heart knew that with Mrs Blair and Clive there would be no cream cookies left over: there would be just one each. I began to hate Clive: if he wasn't here Desmond and I would probably get one and a half cookies each.

Mrs Blair and my parents chatted away as they ate their sandwiches. Clive, head down, ate steadily; my brother and I chewed through our sandwiches slowly, still keeping an eye on the cookies. Clive finished his sandwiches first and my mother, who always had a soft spot for him since his father had died, offered him a cream cookie. With three bites it was gone. We couldn't believe it – he knew nothing about eating cream cookies. My brother and I were still eating our sandwiches. Three more cookies were lifted off the plate and set before Mrs Blair and my mother and father. Halfway through eating hers my mother saw Clive's empty plate. Too late I realised that we had eaten too slowly and before I could swallow the last piece of sandwich my mother lifted the plate with the two cookies – our cookies – and offered them to Clive. Panic and anger were rising in my chest and when he took another one I wanted to kill him. My mother offered the last one to Mrs Blair: with one eye on us and one on Clive she

186

refused. She could count. My mother took a knife and cut the last cream cookie in two and passed over each half to Desmond and me. I didn't know whether to laugh or cry. I've remembered that cream cookie tea all my life.

Whatever friendship might have been between Clive and me was always damaged by the memory of those cream cookies. He became a good friend of my brother but I never told him why I was so cool towards him. He died recently and all I could think of at his funeral was those damned cream cookies.

Yahoo, Ya Boy Ya

PETER BYRNE

"Pete."

"Wha?"

"Wake up."

"Wha?"

"Come on. Get up - you'll be late."

"What time is it?"

"Quarter to six."

"Right."

"Come on, will ya?"

"Okay. Give me a minute."

Opening my eyes my unfamiliar surroundings disorientated my brain. Slowly, it kicked into gear. Angie's bedroom....Angie's parents' house. Sitting up in Angie's bed, I watched her reflected face as she applied make-up in her dressing table mirror. Then my mind wandered, and pondered on the days ahead. This day week we'd be married and on honeymoon: sun, sand and sex. Suddenly my honeymoon was interrupted.

"You go and have a shower, and I'll go down and make breakfast."

Ah, nothing like a cold shower to start a new day......*SCUBY-DE-DO-DA-- SCUBY-DE-DAY-----I'M-SINGING-IN-THE-RAIN—JUST-SINGING-IN- THE-RAIN—WHAT-A-GLORIOUS-FEELING-I-AM-HAP-HAP-HAPEEE- AGAIN----SCUBY-DE-DO-DA—SCUBY-DE- DAY*...

Now where did I leave my clothes?

"Angie. Angie."

"What?"

"Did you see me boxers?"

"Your what – hold on I'll be up. What's wrong with ya – are you not dressed yet?"

188

"I can't find me boxers."

"Your what?"

"Me boxers – me jocks. You know - the things you ripped off me last night."

"You got that the wrong way round, haven't ya?"

"Yahoo, ya girl ya."

"Stop mucking about – they must be there somewhere."

"They're not, I've looked everywhere."

"Did you look under the bed?"

"Under the bed – under the mattress – under the pillow – under the underdown - or should that be eiderdown? Either way I can't find them."

"Look at the time - you'd better hurry up."

"But Angie, I can't go to work without me kecks: me boiler suit would itch the arse off me – not to mention what they'd do to me unmentionables."

"Well try a pair of mine, then."

"What?"

"Me knickers – they're in the top drawer."

"You're joking, aren't you?"

"Why not – who's going to see ya?"

"Okay but -- ah Jasus - are these the only kind you have?"

"What's wrong with them?"

"Nothing – if you're a midget."

"Well you're not exactly King Kong in that department, are ya?"

"Well you weren't complaining last night."

"Excuse me."

"Yahoo, ya girl ya. Seriously though, Angie, I've an eight hour shift to do and I'm not going to be going round cross-eyed – besides, I'd catch my death in them."

"Well I'm afraid that's all I have."

"Are you for real? What do ya wear in the winter?"

"I don't wear any."

"Yahoo, ya girl ya."

"Will you give over?"

189

"Sorry, Angie, but all joking aside, you must have something besides these?"

"Here, what about them?"

"Ah, Jasus - from one extreme to another. Where did you get them?"

"What's wrong with them?"

"Well nothing, if you're into frills and pink, and you're an elephant. Me granny wouldn't be caught dead in them, and she's dead."

"Just put them on, will ya? Look at the time."

"Okay, but one smirk out of you and the wedding's off. So what de ya think?"

"You're gorgeous."

"D'ya think so?"

"Yeah - take a look in the mirror."

"Ah Jasus, Angie - I look a right handbag. Is this all ya have?"

"Take it or leave it. Like I say: who's going to see ya?"

"I suppose... okay then."

"Right, hurry up - breakfast is ready."

After breakfast in Angie's kitchen, I pulled my jacket from the back of a chair and made for the door, then stopped in my tracks when I heard the word – HELLOOOO – from behind me.

"Aren't you forgetting something?"

Angie was tapping her lips with her finger.

"Oh right - a kiss. I'll see you tonight."

"See ya. Drive carefully."

Making my way across Dublin, from the north side to the south side, the taste of toothpaste mixed with marmalade from Angie's lips, concentrated my mind. Then it shifted. Jasus, what if I had an accident. The very thought of anyone seeing me in these drawers put a shiver through my whole body. Slow down. Think of something else. Right. Get this shift over with. Off the weekend. Only Monday, Tuesday and Wednesday to work, then three weeks of freedom. Two of them on honeymoon in the Costa-lot. Freedom's maybe the wrong word; after all I'm getting married. I can see us now, walking down the aisle. Angie, looking drop dead gorgeous in her

190

wedding dress; me in my pink granny knickers. Jasus, enough of that. Radio, turn on - that's better.

Arriving at the factory car park with five minutes to spare, I clocked in and made my way to the locker rooms. I nearly forgot myself. While the rest of the lads were changing into their boiler suits, I slipped into the toilets to do likewise. Ten o'clock tea break came and I needed a pee. Standing at the urinal, I zipped down my boiler suit, but I was struggling - I forgot women don't have a Y in the front of their panties. With a curious look from a fellow workmate I sneaked into a cubicle and began stripping. Jasus, I thought, compared to men women definitely got a raw deal in the plumbing department, and in more ways than one.

The day was going in quick enough. At lunchtime the talk in the canteen was all about Bisto Brady's new Ford Capri.

"Did you get a look at it?" my soon-to-be Best Man asked.

"I didn't, John. I'll have a look when we're finished."

At three o'clock the hooter sounded the end of shift. After changing, everyone made their way to the car park to get a gander at the new Capri. Southsiders and their love affair with cars, I thought, as I tucked my shirt into my jeans, hurrying to catch-up.

"Well, what d'you think of that?" Bisto asked.

"Not bad, I suppose. The colour's shite."

"Shite? That's walnut brown, that is. Expensive."

"More the colour of gravy, if ya ask me."

"You mean like Bisto gravy?" a voice asked.

Everyone laughed except Bisto.

"Very funny lads - but you wouldn't see one of them on the North side, unless it was stolen," Bisto retaliated.

Now everyone was having a laugh at my expense, but I was used to this sort of ribbing, being the only Northsider amongst them.

Then, above the laughing I heard John roar, "Right lads - grab him."

Before I could comprehend what was happening, I was on me back on the ground, with a multitude of hands pulling at my clothes, my feet were in the air and two of them were pulling my shoes off. I struggled, but it was no use. I had an idea they would give me a "doing" on account of getting married, but I wasn't expecting it till next week and only now did I

191

remember what I was wearing under my jeans. I struggled like mad, but it didn't make any difference - there were too many of them. Then suddenly the cheering and banter was replaced by a gasp of silence as a gaggle of heads with open mouths looked down on me. Then all broke into spontaneous convulsions at the sight of me - naked except for the pink granny knickers I was wearing.

"I always knew you Northsiders were a kinky lot," Bisto roared out.

"Give us a gander," little Willie, on the outside of the bunch, chirped, jumping up and down, his head disappearing and reappearing.

"Jasus, I've been sharing a locker room with a tranny for the past two years and I didn't know," Blacky Crowe yelled.

They continued slagging like this and to say I was embarrassed didn't come close. With tears running down their cheeks and their bellies sore from laughing, they carried me out the factory gates and tied me, hands and feet, to a lamppost. Before they disappeared they put a sign above my head: GETTING HITCHED.

A bus passing on the far side of the road slowed down, then came to a sudden stop. The driver was giving his passengers a free show. In every window, upstairs and downstairs, there were faces, all animated. I couldn't hear what they were saying - I didn't have to. It was like looking at a silent film, without the piano music, but the beeping of car horns going past made up for it. When the bus pulled away, three girls my own age came sauntering along. Stopping, they broke into convulsions. Then one of them chuckled.

"Hey, Bernie: would you say he got them knickers in Dunne's Stores or Marks and Spencer's?"

"Ah, Jasus, they'd have to be out of Marks and Sparks, Mary. You wouldn't get the likes of them in Dunne's."

"What do you think, Margaret?"

"I'd say he robbed them off a granny – the dirty faggot."

With that they marched off giggling. Helpless, I resorted to the only weapon I had: my wit.

"Maggie," I shouted after the fat one, "if I had an arse as big as a planet, like you, I wouldn't come out in daylight." Margaret replied by giving me the finger.

192

Then an ould one with a mutt on a lead walked up to me; she looked about ninety.

"Are you all right, son?" she enquired.

"Hey missus - you wouldn't get your dog to chew these ropes for me, would ya?" I was using my wit again to console myself.

"What was that, son?"

"You wouldn't get your dog to chew these ropes," I shouted.

"Sorry son, you'll have to speak up. I'm a little hard of hearing."

Roaring now: "You wouldn't get...." I was interrupted by a warm sensation on my legs. "Ah Jasus, missus. Your dog is pissing on me."

She followed my gaze. "I'm sorry son, but Trixie always stops at this lamp post - it's his favourite one."

I had my mouth open, but I couldn't speak. Adding insult to injury, the scroungy mutt turned his arse to me and began scraping the ground, using his two back paws with gusto and covering my wet legs with dirt and gravel.

"Will you be all right, son?"

I couldn't answer her.

"Will I get you a coat for over your shoulders? You must be freezing."

"No missus – I'm working on me tan."

"What was that you said, son?"

"I'm working on me bleeding tan," I roared, to which she replied, "You're waiting on a van? Okay then, son. I'll see ya so."

Just when I thought things couldn't get much worse, a gang of four young fellas on bikes stopped. They were munching on ice pops, in between jeering and laughing.

"I dare you to put your ice pop down his knickers," one said to another.

"You do and I'll kick your hole for ya." I thought attack would be my best defence. I was wrong.

"Don't mind him - sure his legs are tied," another one squawked.

With that, the smallest of them - a scruffy-faced little runt - jumped off his bike, took a big bite from the top of his ice pop, and pulling the elastic of me knickers out as far as they'd stretch, spat it down into them, letting the elastic fling back, slapping me belly. The cold made my eyes water and my lips whistled in reverse.

193

"Ya little bollox," I managed to shout after him, as he took off with the rest of his friends, all yelling and yahooing like a bunch of Indians who had just taken a scalp.

Where the ice had melted, a damp patch appeared, making my manhood visible or maybe invisible since my buddy down below had been shrivelled and frozen. And judging by a comment made by one of the many passers-by, he had. In this case a woman, bleached blonde and proud, impressing her younger friend.

"Cocktail sausages are fine if you're peckish, but no use if you're famished. It's the big sausage you want for that, if you follow me, Sharon."

"Oh I do, Sasha....I do."

"Sharon," I whispered under my breath after her, "I hope the wire in your bra punctures your tits."

Then something twigs the corner of me eye and when I look round, I see this road sweeper standing on the kerb. Without a word, he joins his hands, places them on top of his brush shaft and rests his chin on them. After a long time studying me, he eventually opens his mouth.

"Do you work in there?"

"I do, yeah."

"What's the money like?"

"Well, mm, pretty good."

"How much do you take home?"

"Two hundred."

"A week?"

"Yeah."

"What do you have to do for that?"

"Well, its shifts and....."

"Shifts?...Ah, fuck that," he says and disappears down the street, pushing his brush.

Eventually John and a few of the lads arrived back and untied me. They were trying to keep from laughing as they handed me my clothes but I was gone beyond caring or trying to explain how I came to be wearing pink knickers in the first place.

That evening I drove round to Angie's house. She was all dressed up and putting the finishing touches to her make-up.

"Are we going out?" I enquired.

"Yeah - thought we might go down the local, since it's our last night of sin."

For the past week, Angie's parents had been on holiday in the sun, getting a colour to look good for their only daughter's wedding day. Angie and me were having our own holiday in her parent's home, getting some practice in for married life. We didn't get much sun.

"Okay," I said, "but I'm not going to the local – we'll head into town."

"Right, then: town it is."

Sitting in the Parnell Mooney, Angie was telling me how her parents were getting on but I wasn't listening.

"Don't forget we're picking them up from the airport tomorrow."

"Who?"

"My mother and father – are you listening to me at all?"

Not being able to contain myself any longer, I blurted out, "Jasus, Angie – I don't believe you let me wear them knickers."

"Why? What happened?"

"You don't want to know."

"Tell me."

"Ah, forget it."

"No – tell me."

"Okay, but promise you won't laugh."

"I promise."

I began telling her the story but the more I went into it the louder she laughed.

"Jasus, Angie – it's no laughing matter. D'ya not realise all me workmates think I'm kinky?"

She had a mouthful of gin and she blurted it out all over the carpet.

"It's not bleeding funny – how am I going to face them on Monday?"

It was no use: when Angie took a fit of the giggles there was no talking to her. I noticed we were attracting attention from some of the other customers and overheard a bloke in a blazer, at another table, educating his company with his knowledge of drugs.

195

"That's the effect smoking pot has on a person."

"Will you keep it down?" I snapped, but this only made her worse.

I went to the bar to get us another drink, only to get a mouthful from the barman. "Will you keep it down over there?"

When I got back to our table I told Angie to pull herself together or she'd get us barred. But this only sent her into more kinks although she did manage to say through her teeth, "What did John say?"

"John who? Oh, you mean John - me supposedly best man? Lot of good he was – it was him who put the rest of them up to it."

On hearing this she jumped up and made a dash for the toilets, squeaking as she went, "I think I'm going to wet meself."

When she came back she was more composed.

"Well," I said, "did you ever find me boxers?"

With that she went into hysterics again, at the same time pulling me boxers from her handbag and holding them up.

"You mean these?" she spluttered.

"Where did you find them?" I asked, but she couldn't reply from laughing. Then the barman arrived with a bouncer at his side.

"I'm going to have to ask you two to leave," he ordered.

"Ah, Jasus – what harm is she doing?"

"She's annoying the other customers – come on out."

"Ah, Jasus lads – she's annoying me, too. But what can I tell yas - I'm having a bad day."

As soon as I had it out, Angie went into a fit of uncontrolled laughter, even worse than before.

"Okay, okay – we're going. Come on you," I shouted.

Tripping in her high heels, Angie's laughter could be heard all the way down Parnell Street and half way up O'Connell Street to the taxi rank. Sitting in the back of the taxi, with a grumpy head, I reluctantly spoke to my giggling partner.

"I don't know how you find it so funny - after all, people are going to say you're marrying a transvestite."

Wiping tears mixed with mascara from her face, she blurted, "Have you not copped on yet?"

"Copped on? Copped on? Copped on to what? Hold on - what are you saying? Are you saying I was stitched up?"

She couldn't say anything. Instead she shook her head up and down.

"You mean you hid me jocks and gave me them granny ones to wear and John and the rest of the lads were in on it?"

Tears continued down her cheeks, as she shook her head frantically.

"Jasus. You bitch," was all I could manage.

The taxi took us to our local. When we went through the door a big cheer went up. Most of my workmates were there along with some of Angie's friends. It was obvious the whole pub was in on it. John, my best man, came over, carrying a pint.

"You're late," he said, grinning. "Here, get that into ya."

Then Angie took my face in her two hands. "D'you know what?" she said.

"What?"

"You're a big eejit. D'you know that? But I love ya."

After she finished kissing me full on the lips, she roared aloud, "Yahoo, ya boy ya!"

197

Contributors

Anthony Brady was born in London of Co Tyrone mother. Lived in France and Belgium and now in Tempo. Worked as a local government officer in London. Had poems published in Forward Press anthologies and stories in *Ireland's Own* and *Ireland's Eye*. His trilogy *Scenes From An Examined Life* is on www.authonomy.com.

Ian Butler began writing creatively in 2008 after a stroke in England. His social work experience includes working with high risk adolescents. Has had work published in the local Fermanagh papers, various professional journals and the BBC website. He was shortlisted for the prestigious Northern Ireland Screen's Primetime Award. His first novel is scheduled to be launched in 2012.

Peter Byrne is from North Dublin. Has lived in Co Fermanagh for over 20 years and represented the county in the National UK Anthology with his poem *Portora Castle*. He intends to publish his first book of humorous short stories before the end of the year.

Seamus Carolan was born in Clones, Co Monaghan and spent an idyllic childhood on the family farm near Roslea, Co Fermanagh. He was educated in St Columb's College, Derry, and St Joseph's Teacher Training College, Belfast. He spent thirty-two years as a teacher in St Eugene's College, Roslea. Since retiring from teaching he has worked as an architectural consultant.

Mariette Connor was born in Blackrock, Co Dublin. She lived abroad for many years and returned from Spain to retire in Fermanagh in 2003. She has had stories and articles published in newspapers, magazines, and anthologies in Spain, the UK and Ireland.

Grainne Farrell is 20 years old. She has always loved reading and writing and is currently studying at South West College. She hopes to begin a degree in English and Creative Writing in September.

Wayne Hardman is a blow-in from Canada who writes ice hockey reports for newspapers and magazines. He writes stories and autobiography for FCWG. His style is different: he's basically a hockey puck who writes.

John Llewelyn James was a daydreamer and storyteller as a child and left it all behind to embrace mundane reality as an adult. Circumstances allowed him to leave reality behind again and, given the current predilection for dead poets, he harbours the faint hope that his poems may have a life after his own.

Diane Jardel is originally from London. Had poems published in *The Poetic Bond* and *Pen 10 Compendium*. Now lives in Enniskillen and is a founding member of FCWG. See: http://themomentiseternal.webs.com & http://storiesspace.com/courage2bfree.

Dermot Maguire is a retired teacher. In 2005 he published a history of his own place in Fermanagh: *Drumlone At The Crossroads*. He has written for *The Spark* Border Counties History review, which he now edits. He attended Claire Keegan's workshops and highly recommends them.

Katharine May was born in Belfast in 1961. After graduating from Trinity College, Dublin in 1985 she lived in London for 6 years. Received a Masters in Fine Art, as a mature student, from the University of Ulster in 2008. Mainly works in video and writing accompanies her art practice.

Angela McCabe lives in Ballinamore, Co. Leitrim where she works as a psychologist. She also comes from a visual art background, having specialised in Performance Art, appearing in shows worldwide. She has made an award winning short movie and is currently at work on a second one. She is also working on a book of poetry.

Thomas McGovern lives outside Enniskillen and is a fan of genre fiction, especially mystery and crime fiction. He is also a big cinema fan and has previously dabbled in screenplay writing.

Frankie McPhillips lives in Tempo. Has had many articles on fly-fishing and fly-tying published in angling magazines. His early interest in fishing led him to owning a fishing tackle business which he runs in Enniskillen's Buttermarket.

Ken Ramsey is a native of Enniskillen who has always been involved in literature, mostly as a reader. Some years ago he started writing short stories.

Dianne Trimble is an urban Canadian who has settled in rural Northern Ireland. Her articles and stories have featured in Irish and Canadian magazines. Her novel *Hitler and Mars Bars* was released in 2008. Online she lurks at www.dianneascroft.wordpress.com.

Cait Vallely – like many Irish people – had to emigrate, first to England, then Scotland and then to Spain where she lived for over thirty years before returning to Ireland. After living in Galway and Roscommon she has now found her niche in Leitrim.

Anthony Viney is a social worker, originally from London. He enjoys writing short stories with an historical angle. After a recent visit to Syria he has just completed his first novel – an action-packed thriller set during the Arab Spring.

Gordon Williams was born near Manchester when the M6 was still cobbled. Has lived in Fermanagh since 1984. Had articles published in fishing magazines – none are still in business – and stories in the *Sunday Telegraph* magazine, *Ireland's Own, Writing,* and several websites and anthologies.